The very first cover of Breaking Ember, illustrated by
Nick Laney in 2019

This book is for all of the girls who became their own knight in shining armor.

Chapter 1

The sun was beginning to rise, the land covered in a blanket of fresh, white mist. The usual scent of morning dew was floating about and instantly welcomed by the princess's senses. She drifted in and out of her thoughts, watching as leaves fluttered in the wind and birds whooshed by the tower. Free. Clenching her eyes shut, she savored the faint rays of sunlight caressing her skin and the wind brushing against her face before backing away from the window. She told herself the outside world was a dangerous and formidable place, but in her mind, she secretly disagreed with herself.

Celestia had been locked in a tower for nearly her whole life. She didn't have many childhood memories and absolutely no *human* friends. In fact, it had been so long since she had interacted with another human being, they had nearly become mythical creatures to her. Even the images of her family were warped in her mind; She couldn't help but wonder if they looked anything like her.

Being somewhere around the age of twenty, the princess was itching to explore the world beyond the tower. All she wanted was the chance to have a little taste of life before she perished and became just a faint memory. That is, if there was even anyone left to remember her anymore.

She sank down to the floor, running her fingers through her hair and placing her head in her hands. How could she continue to live like this? The day faded so easily into night, the trees shed their leaves every autumn and started anew in the spring. The world functioned in a never ending cycle that started over again, each and every year. She loathed the world and how it could move on with such grace and beauty while she was stuck here, doing and being nothing. If the world could even move.. wasn't it flat last she checked?

Even if it was, that didn't change anything. She'd never get to see the edge of the world, she'd never be able to venture away from her awful tower; Her dragon was set on making her stay.

A snout peaked in through the window, pulling the princess from her morbid thoughts and causing her lips to pull into a grin. She lifted herself off the floor and made her way over to her dragon's head, petting it softly. He dropped a basket of apples at her feet, and her stomach growled in thanks almost immediately.

"Abaven, you mustn't leave me for so long! It gets rather boring without having you around," she proclaimed, snatching fruit from the basket and sinking her teeth into it's juicy flesh. She heard a deep rumble from within his throat and knew immediately he was defending himself.

'I would love to hang around all day, but I have to get you food to eat!' he seemed to say. The princess shook her head, smiling slightly. Her smile didn't stay for long, though, and that worried Abaven. He watched her silently as her eyebrows clenched together in thought and knew immediately what troubled her.

As if to say 'You know your father placed you here to protect you,' Abaven nudged the princess with his snout. His bright green eyes locked with her own and she nodded her head and rolled her eyes. That was a response she was used to from him; even Abaven didn't have a clue as to why she was there! He knew he had to protect her, and he knew he had to keep her hidden until the king returned. But it had been a decade and a half since she had been locked away and there was no sign of the king returning anytime soon. The princess was sick of wondering every day why her father had left her in a tower so far away. She hated pondering what things her father could have possibly been protecting her from. What about the world outside could possibly be so bad?

Abaven rested his head on the floor, pulling his mouth into what could be mistaken as a snarl but the princess recognized it as a smile. The princess sat down next to his head, leaning softly on his snout and enjoying his presence.

Nestling comfortably by her dragon, the princess was taken back to the day her parents had sent her away; the day her childhood had ended and her world had changed.

"Wake up!" The king spoke gingerly, rocking the dozing girl. She yawned, stretching her limbs and smiling drowsily at her father. His worried eyes gazed at her fondly, haltingly managing to grip his daughter's hand and yank her from beneath the covers. He pulled her alongside him, his angst growing every time she tripped over her feet.

They rushed down the palace stairs, the small princess just barely becoming aware of her surroundings. The king stared ahead grimly, unable to meet his daughter's eyes. He still hadn't the slightest idea if what he was doing was right; There was a possibility he may never see her again. As he pondered this thought, he realized it was for the best. As long as his daughter was safe, he would be alright with the consequences that would follow.

The palace doors were quickly opened for them and the queen stood waiting, clutching a small child in her arms as tears coursed down her cheeks. The little princess gazed at her worriedly.

"Mommy, are you okay?" The young girl whispered, her voice hushed and quavering. Her mother tenderly grabbed her hand, gazing down at her through teary eyes. With one last heart-wrenching glance at the little girl, her mother let go and turned away. The little princess worriedly watched as her mother walked through the palace doors, wondering where her mother was going.

The king embraced his daughter, looking deeply into her eyes before leading her to a horse-drawn carriage. He picked her up, smiling at her one last time before handing her to one of the waiting servants.

"Where am I going, daddy? Are you coming?" The king shook his head.

"You're not safe here, darling. These men will take you somewhere safe. I can't come with you, I have to protect the people in my kingdom. But I will come to get you one day, okay?"

The little princess nodded, unable to comprehend what was happening. But before she got the chance to ask her father where she was going, and why she wasn't safe, she was shut in the carriage. She could hear the clacking of horse hooves on the cobblestone road and her father quickly disappeared behind her.

Thoughts plagued the princess: questions that still remained unanswered, her longing for the family dissipating from her memory, and the desire to delve into the world beyond her tower began to burn within her.

Chapter 2

The princess paced her room, trying hard to think of something interesting to occupy her time. Failing, she flopped onto the silky smooth cushions of her welcoming bed. Today was one of the few days she was able to refrain from the yearning to inspect the world outside her window.

She hummed a song to herself, lacing her fingers together and flailing her feet in the air. As all who have been locked in a tower know, boredom is a dangerous and unnerving feeling. The only solution for this princess, in particular, was a book. The princess shoved her hand under her satin pillow, digging through the cotton and silk until she felt the torn binding of her ancient novel. Her eyes dropped to its now visible cover.

It was the only book that she had managed to preserve during her many years in the tower and the one thing she always turned to on her loneliest days. Although the princess could not read very well, as her education had stopped when she had been relocated to the tower, she had memorized the tale from when her mother used to read it to her. If she had been asked, she could recite the entire book word for word. She cracked it open to the first chapter, the lovely scent of old paper immediately welcomed by her senses. It was probably her favorite smell.

"Once Upon A Time..." if only she was in a fairytale, where dreams came true. Where there was automatically a happy ending and a chance to roam free. After scanning over the first few pages and taking particular notice of the pictures on every one, the princess abandoned the book, placing it down and casting her eyes toward the ceiling. She loved imagining the way townsfolk interacted, and how knights and fair maidens romanced each other, but today she just couldn't seem to focus on the story. The pictures jumbled together in her brain, becoming one confusing mass of scenes. It was becoming harder to pretend she knew how humans interacted normally with one another when the only social interaction she had was with a mythical (and yet very real) creature.

The princess rolled off the bed, her feet hitting the cold stone floor and sending shivers up her spine. She pulled her robe more tightly around herself and glided to the windowsill, which sat to the left of her bed. Her eyes were drawn to the clouds rolling through the sky, turning a majestic shade of gold as the sun began to set. As she gazed out the window, she realized her life was much like a fairytale itself (despite the lack of a charming prince). She was a princess whose dearest friend was a dragon, stationed in a tower, and doomed to wither away eternally. Although she could very easily leave with Abaven, she lived in her tower because she believed her father would return to beckon her home, or a hunky hero would arrive to carry her off into the sunset. If that didn't seem like a fairytale, she didn't know what did!

Celestia was reminded, then, that she had not spent the entirety of the past decade and a half *in the tower*. Although it took a very long time to convince her dragon, a couple of years after she had arrived at the tower she had managed to persuade him into taking her flying.

After much deliberation, Abaven finally agreed to allowing Celestia to ride his back while he flew around the tower a couple of times. Celestia, excitedly, stood up on her window ledge and waited for Abaven to meet her level. She jumped onto his back as he rose, and her small hands gripped onto Abaven's spinal scales. She giggled in delight, her heart rate quickening as she excitedly realized they were now floating above the tower.

More than anything, she loved the feeling of the wind caressing her face and the pungent scent of the earth after a fresh rain that hung in the air. Celestia caught glimpses of tiny rivers and trees below her, scenery that stretched on for miles and miles. Clouds floated peacefully around her and Abaven, sprinkling her with mist as they flapped through them.

She could see so much more than she could from her window! The world was so much bigger than she could ever comprehend; it was beautiful.

It wasn't until the last loop around the tower that Celestia realized wearing a dress while riding a dragon had been a bad idea. Her legs were rubbed raw from friction, small trails of blood trickling between each ebony scale of the dragon. Sudden pain flashed through her eyes as the adrenaline was finally fading.

Her hands clamped onto the scales and she fought the discomfort... but it didn't leave. She desired more than anything to feel the wind in her hair and soak in the sight of the world around her, but soon the pain became unbearable. Her grip was slipping, and if she didn't speak up soon, she would fall.

"S-stop!" she called out, causing Abaven to look back at her. Immediately, he swooped downwards and landed softly on the grass beside her tower. She sighed thankfully, only for her breath to hitch in her throat; each breath she took was painful. Her lungs tightened and her chest heaved up and down frantically, her heart strained.

Abaven slightly stretched his wings, tilting to the side and allowing Celestia's weight to shift to his left. The fabric-like material of the wing barely bent as Celestia's tiny body slid down. She rolled onto the ground, softly falling onto her back.

Grass hugged her skin, her dress tumbling over their sharp blades and squashing them beneath the crusted fabric, caked with blood. Abaven dropped onto his stomach, lowering himself beside Celestia. Pulling his arms and legs to his side, he faced her. He stretched his wings slightly and rested his head in the grass beside her. His tail wagged back and forth, proof he truly believed she'd get up and smile, laugh, or even stretch.

"Abaven, I can't move," she whimpered, staring blankly up at him as the grass was further stained with her blood. Abaven's tail lowered and the actuality of the moment struck him. He scooted closer to her and then curled his tail around her, encasing her in a circle. He couldn't stand to see Celestia in pain and this was all he could do to heal her.

Lowering his snout next to her head, he cast her one anxious glance before licking the blood from her legs and the scrapes that lined her arms. Blood no longer flowed from her body, the layer of saliva preventing any further bleeding. The skin beneath slowly began to scab over once more, repairing itself with the help of the dragons magic.

Allowing a puff of smoke to escape from between his teeth in satisfaction, he retracted his head, lying tiredly beside Celestia. He cast one last glimpse at her before his eyes shut. The magic had drained him and no matter how much he wished he could stay awake, he couldn't. His wings lowered over the both of them, providing a shield from the chilly air and the dangers beyond the clearing.

Celestia was unable to fall asleep and stared up at the sky through a gap in between Abaven's wings. The day had finally begun to fade into night, and stars peeped from beneath the bed of clouds as the golden hues faded quickly away and were replaced with darkness. In minutes, the setting sun had turned into a starry night sky. The moon shone bright and full, serving as a centerpiece in the midst of the painting.

As she lay there staring up at the beautiful night sky, her thoughts returned to her first flight with Abaven.

From her perch atop her dragon, the scenery had seemed to shrink while the world around her expanded. When she was looking out her tower window, Celestia could only see the meadow beneath her and the tips of the trees surrounding it. But up there, from Abaven's back, she could see rolling hills and twisting rivers. There were even mountains far off in the distance; so much more to see than she had ever imagined. When she was flying with Abaven, she felt a sense of freedom that sitting in her tower had never brought her, a feeling as though all limits had disappeared.

The pain in her legs gradually lessened, and the chilly blanket of night air beckoned her to sleep. As her eyes began to droop, her mind was plagued with blurring thoughts. Now that she had a glimpse of the enormity of the world around her, she only wanted to see more of it. But Abaven had told her that some of the most beautiful things were also the most dangerous. Celestia finally came to the conclusion that the allure of nature was deceiving. Even though she longed to explore the world around her, she would retreat to her tower first thing in the morning.

Celestia looked out the window, admiring the same sky she had that fateful night. The stars were a reminder of the horizons she had yet to reach and explore.

Her fascination with the stars hadn't begun that night with Abaven, however. She could faintly remember nights spent with her parents on the hills beside their palace, searching the skies for constellations and numbering the stars. Their kingdom was governed through calculations and predictions originated from the stars. Her parents had even named her Celestia, knowing full well she would spend her life searching the heavens and counting the stars because of it.

The stars gave her hope that someday she wouldn't have to wait for her father or her prince charming, she would be able to brave the world on her own.

Chapter 3

"Clifton, Look!" Borin exclaimed, his thick country accent barely comprehensible. His hand, scarred with the marks of a million battles, was pointed toward a faint grey shape rising in the distance. Borin and Thomas had accompanied Sir Clifton in search of this very landmark for what seemed like years. Clifton focused his eyes in the direction Borin was pointing and his lips stretched into an exultant smile. They had finally found it! Pulling the reins of his steed he bolted forward, his companions trailing afterward.

As the pounding of hooves and soft neighs further closed the distance, the faint shape visibly changed into a stone tower. Vines twisted in and out of its stones, holding them forcibly in place over the years. The four men continued forward without doubt or fear, exhilaration evident in their movements. The swords latched to their belts swung dangerously with each step their horses took; cold air whipped past them, causing their extravagant capes to billow behind them as they rode.

Sir Clifton pulled the reins that were gripped tightly in his hands, forcing his horse to a stop. A soft melody drifted from the tower and he cupped his ear with his gloved hand, trying to capture each note of the sweet song and savoring its alluring tune. His blue eyes glittered with astonishment. Combing a hand through his sun-streaked locks, he jumped from his steed, landing with a thud. He now knew his journey hadn't been in vain!

For months Sir Clifton and his men had searched for a tower rumored to be much like this one, containing what he hoped was a princess singing within its walls. Prince Lucier had sent several parties searching for this princess with the promise of unimaginable riches, enough to last them ten lifetimes, and a pick of any land in his kingdom if they brought her back to him. Lucky for them, their party had gotten there first. The princess was theirs for the taking, they were going to be rich!

Although Clifton would not say it aloud, he thought Prince Lucier to be a narcissistic and cowardly ruler over their kingdom. He was too scared to search for the princess himself and bribed nobles into doing the dirty work for him. Clifton wondered, for a brief second, what Prince Lucier wanted with a maiden so far West, he had his pick of any woman in the kingdom and instead decided he wanted none of them. Whatever the reason was, Clifton forced himself not to care. He was not here to rescue the princess, he was here to acquire and deliver her to the Prince so he could obtain his reward.

Eagerly, Clifton raced forward and upon nearing the tower he leaped high to grasp the thick, trailing vines. Lifting his weight, he continued upwards. He didn't dare to look down, his mind was focused only on reaching the top. Borin, always one to follow Clifton, ran after him and began to climb the tower as well.

Thomas rolled his eyes as he watched them ascend towards the top. Nobody was as impulsive as Lord Clifton or as foolish a follower as Borin. There had to have been some easier way to reach the princess than climbing the tower! Thomas began searching the base of the tower for a ladder or, better yet, a set of stairs. He succeeded, opening a latched door and making his way up the tower at a much quicker rate than his companions.

But they had all forgotten the one thing Prince Lucier had warned them of; the beast that guarded her. Which isn't something one should forget.

From inside the tower, Celestia could hear thumping and clumping, voices swinging in and out of earshot. Curiously, she peered over the edge of her windowsill, only to find the eyes of two peculiar men staring up at her.

Quickly she swung back into the room, stumbling toward her desk in search of some sort of weapon. People were climbing her tower? Where was a dragon when you needed him?! Grabbing the hardest object she could find, a crumbling stone jutting from the wall, she walked cautiously toward the window. Her fingers delicately traced the stone's rough edges, her heart thumping rhythmically with each quivering breath.

Behind her, the door to her room flew open and a large man stepped into the room. Celestia screamed, she was under attack! Immediately, without so much as a thought, the stone flew out of Celestia's hand and thwacked the man in the head.

He stumbled, falling forward onto the floor in front of her with a large thump.

Panicked, Celestia knelt on the floor beside him, flipping him onto his back and staring down at his motionless face. Had she just killed a man?

Upon further observation of the body, her eyes caught a glimpse of the glistening sword in his belt, and she immediately recalled the book she had read previously that week. Wait. What if these men were here to free her? What if they were her chance of escape? What if one of them was her prince charming? Although it was probably a stupid thing to do, she allowed hope to swell throughout her chest. Her hand hovered over his mouth and, as she felt his hot breath against her skin, she was filled with relief. He wasn't dead!

Screams echoed through the air, drawing her attention away from the man lying on her floor and causing her to peek once more out the window. Horses galloped rapidly away from the area, struggling to reach the safety of the woods. A man was lying limp in the jaws of her dragon and another had already descended from the tower and unsheathed his sword. Her dragon growled at him, revealing his pointed teeth. The second man, obviously terrified out of his mind, realized he had no chance of fighting that dragon alone. He heedlessly chucked his dagger at Abaven in hope of a distraction. The dagger pierced her beast's leg and sent a roar of pain echoing through the valley. Before her beast could catch him, the man had disappeared into the dense woods, the only trace of his presence was the bloody blade lying on the grass.

Abaven retreated back to the tower, grinding his blood-stained teeth with displeasure. He couldn't believe that in the mere few minutes he had gone hunting for food, intruders had arrived! Despite the pain in his leg from the dagger's cut, his first instinct was to check on Celestia, hoping she was alright. Abaven spread his wings and effortlessly lifted himself into the air, latching on to the side of the tower and looking into Celestia's window. He took immediate notice of the man behind Celestia and squinted his eyes as if to say 'Move, Celestia'.

Celestia slid away from the window, allowing Abaven to stick his snout in and grab the man lying on her floor.

"What if these men were here to bring me back to my father, Abaven? What if they didn't mean any harm?" But Celestia's persistent questions didn't stop her dragon from dragging the man out of Celestia's window. Abaven looked back at Celestia, who gazed at him helplessly.

Abaven's voice hastily entered Celestia's thoughts: 'These men were not here to free you, Celestia. They were here to kidnap you and hold you for ransom. These men are exactly what I'm here to protect you from!' With that, Abaven and the man in his jaws disappeared around the side of the tower.

Celestia stared after him, resting her arms on the window sill. Her hair glittered in the sun, creating a heavenly aura around her restless soul. Tears glistened in her eyes, her gaze moving to the birds flapping by and the trees dancing with the wind. Unbound. Which she could never be. No chance of exploring the outside world. No chance of adventure.

Celestia's mind was filled with bitter thoughts towards her dragon for keeping her there, but her heart reminded her it was because he cared about her. He had endangered himself to keep her safe. She wondered then if he was alright; had the dagger pierced him deeply?

Lucky enough, Abaven had barely been scratched by the sword. Only tiny drops of black ooze escaped the wound on his leg. As the ooze began to dry, he stretched his long neck and rose to his hind legs. Abaven leaned his forearms against the tower, resting his black scales against the cold bricks and taking notice of the princess slouched tiredly against the window sill.

Flying upwards, he reached the level of the window and poked his head into the tower. He gently pushed a sleepy Celestia from the windowsill and onto his snout, nudging her onto the fluffy folds of her bed. Even if she hated him then, he would never stop caring for her. He withdrew his head from the tower, slowly allowing himself to descend to the grassy meadow below once more.

Celestia's eyes watched drowsily as Abaven's glistening black scales had disappeared from sight. She burrowed into the silky blankets on her bed, examining her room and thinking of life outside the tower.

"*Some day,*" She reasoned with herself. Once again, she fell asleep, dreaming of princes and dragons and the happily ever after she'd never have.

Chapter 4

In truth, Celestia knew that her hunger would never be filled; it wasn't her stomach that longed for sustenance. But it was always easier to fill her mouth than her soul. Since Celestia had not yet eaten breakfast, she scoured the room for something edible. As she caught a glimpse of red, her stomach rumbled in gratefulness. She hurriedly grabbed the bright crimson apple lying beside her and hungrily sunk her teeth into its juicy flesh, savoring that first, crisp bite. She felt as though she hadn't eaten in days and rapidly devoured the red fruit.

Once there was nothing left but a slender core, she absent-mindedly made her way towards her dresser. As was part of her daily routine, she began brushing through her tangled hair, wincing as the knots unsnarled with each slide of the brush. Sometimes her hair seemed a little too long for her liking; it felt like a constant weight on her head and was always in knots and tangles. But even still, she could remember when her mother used to comb and braid her hair on chilly summer evenings back at her kingdom. Her father always had a liking for her hair, and always complimented her on its length and beauty. Losing the length of her hair would almost be like breaking a connection with her parents, which would result in her losing hope that she would see them again. Hope that her father would return for her someday.

Celestia then realized that keeping her hair long to play along with the fairytale-like fantasy that her father would come to rescue her was misguided and foolish. If she were ever going to escape from the tower, she would need to do so herself.

Shifting her gaze to the dresser mirror, Celestia gathered the curly strands of gold from her face and tied her unruly hair in a loose ponytail. Her sharp gaze flashed across her dresser, landing on the little pile of sewing supplies at the back. She reached over, pushing aside fabrics, spindles, and sewing needles until she found what she desired.

The first step to her freedom would be to cut off her long, tangled knots of disheveled hair.

Her hand briefly hovered above the scissors before she seized them and, in one quick flash of the silver shears, her ponytail was lying on the floor beside her feet. As she glanced back at the mirror, she reached up to touch her blonde locks, which now waved gently around her face, ending just at her chin. Her appearance wasn't the only thing that had changed, she felt like a weight had been lifted from her soul. She no longer felt like a helpless princess who waited for life to happen to her, she looked like the type of girl who would finally take charge of her own destiny.

She couldn't help but jump up and twirl around, her gaze flickering towards the mirror and admiring how each new action made her feel so much more free. With the word 'free' piercing her thoughts, she quickly moved forward then stopped in front of the door that led out of the tower.

She recalled the endless evenings she'd spent gazing at that door, knowing that Abaven would never let her leave the tower and so it was up to her to take action. So many times over the years she had grown so restless that she opened the door and fled down the stairs, only to find that the door at the bottom was locked.

But that man, the one she had (accidentally) knocked out with a rock... he had come up the stairs so he had opened the door. Maybe it was still unlocked?

Brushing long vines of ivy away from the frame, her hand traced over the door's black iron handle. Her heart seemed to bang against her chest, threatening to break free.

She would go outside. What was the point of sitting by and waiting for Prince Charming, when she could save herself? Why attempt to convince Abaven to let her run free when he only ever said no? She *wasn't* in a fairytale. This was reality, and she'd finally come to this realization.

Slowly, her fingers wrapped around the handle, gripping it tightly. The door opened with a long, deafening creak. The hall beyond her was pitch black, the spiraling stone stairs barely visible in the darkness. She took no time to look back at the room behind her, and stepped forward as the door closed, leaving her in the shadows with a soft click. Feeling along the cold stones, she gradually began her descent down the stairs. Her bare toes curling at the temperature change. Although she couldn't see, she had long ago memorized the placement of each step and her feet moved swiftly and with assurance. Not once did Celestia stop to find her footing, she knew exactly where she was going and exactly what waited for her at the end.

Nothing could stop her from obtaining her freedom, even if it were only for a day.

Celestia trailed her hand along the wall at the base of the stairway until she arrived at the huge wooden door which led outside. Grasping the metal handle, she closed her eyes and made one quick wish, a wish for the chance at freedom. She quickly pressed down on the handle, fully expecting it to remain firmly locked, but she felt the handle give and then heard the firm click of the lock disengaging. A shaft of sunlight burst through the edge of the frame as the heavy wooden door inched open. Leaving the door slightly ajar, she blinked repeatedly, adjusting her eyes to the brightness. She glanced at the black tail, propped in front of the door and acting as a weight. Her dragon's large snout was barely visible on the other side of the tower, soft streams of smoke escaping each nostril. Taking that as a sign Abaven was sleeping soundly, she slipped from the door, tiptoeing through the spiky blades of grass and avoiding him completely.

After her first obstacle was avoided, Celestia took the time to observe the outside world's features and delicacy. The flowers in the field were so much more beautiful up close, she noted. She quietly plucked a few from the grass, sniffing them as she slowly continued forward. She dug her toes into the ground and scooped up handfuls of dirt, eyeing it peculiarly. She relished the feeling of earth beneath her feet and had never felt more alive. Even though she knew that if Abaven awoke, and found her standing there, he would be infuriated, she couldn't help but twirl around in glee. She had never felt so alive a single day in that tower as she did right then.

Thinking back to her confined days in the tower, she glanced back over her shoulder toward the tower... But Abaven wasn't there.

Swallowing the lump in her throat, she slowly turned her head forward and clamped her eyes shut. Lifting an eyelid, she tilted her head, peering directly into the yellow, cat-like eyes of her dragon.

"I know you're angry, and you have told me countless times that I can't wander out of this tower because it is my only barrier from the evils of this world," Celestia stopped, glancing down at a flower she held clenched in her fist.

"After looking out my window for the past 15 years, I have seen nothing other than beauty. I've watched as baby deer grew and listened as birds sang. I've watched flowers bloom in the spring and snow fall in the winter. The world can't possibly be as evil as you think."

She looked up, eyeing the clouds above her and the trees around her. "Abaven, I can't keep living a life of nothing."

Abaven looked down at her and knew immediately that she would never be content in this tower. He knew his purpose was to protect her but now realized that maybe he didn't have to keep her locked up in order to do so. When he had first been placed by Celestia's father in that meadow, he had assumed that guarding the tower would always be his duty. But maybe it was never about keeping Celestia cooped up in that tower. What if he and Celestia had a greater purpose outside of that meadow?

Abaven could remember the King's exact words to him when he had been brought to the tower two decades prior. "In a few years time, I will be placing my daughter Celestia here, in your care. I need you to keep her safe and protect her from a man named Lucier. Keep her company and make sure she is happy and healthy. Please, protect her with your life if you have to. I cannot return to this tower until I know it is safe; I have to keep the location of this tower hidden. When the time is right, I will either come to retrieve her myself, or send someone for her; someone I trust."

But the King couldn't possibly have meant for her to spend the entirety of her life in that tower? What if he never came to retrieve her... what if it was never safe?

Celestia looked up at him, waiting patiently for his response. After several minutes of silence, he looked her in the eye and gave her a curt nod. The world may never be safe enough for Celestia, but Abaven would be by her side as they braved their way through it.

Celestia smiled, turning on her heel and looking over her shoulder to say:

"Abaven, we need to begin preparation to leave this tower. We can't keep waiting for someone to come and rescue us, we have to take these matters into our own hands."

With that, Celestia started towards the tower. She entered the hallway and the door slammed shut behind her. Retreating up the stairs, she became more excited with every step closer to the top of the stairwell.

Her toes curled at the feeling of wood beneath her feet, so familiar but suddenly so much less appealing than earth. Upon reaching her room, Celestia closed the door behind her and immediately got to work.

She sent Abaven to collect food: nuts, berries, herbs, and any other non-perishable aliments he could find. While waiting for him to return she started grabbing durable fabrics, animal hides from past meals, and old, frilly dresses, cutting and sewing until she was able to make apparel much more suitable for a journey on dragon-back. Her labor had resulted in three sets of trousers and tunics, along with a thick, black cloak.

Celestia, upon finishing her sewing, scoured the room for anything she could use to her aid. She grabbed a dagger, which she had taken from the man who had snuck into her tower and proceeded to gather together her sewing supplies, in case she would need to repair her clothing. Searching a little longer, she was even able to find an old pair of shoes!

Finally, she retired for the night, proud of her proficiency. She was nearly ready! Celestia found herself smiling gayly in realization...

She would finally have her freedom.

Chapter 5

Ducking underneath her bed, Celestia felt around in the shadows. As soon as her hands brushed against an object, she pulled it out. Staring at a decaying apple, she curled her face in disgust, throwing it immediately across the room. How long had that been under her bed? She decided she'd rather not know and continued her search.

Her fingers brushed something wedged against the wall. She gripped the edge and pulled it out from beneath the bed. Sighing in relief, she began to stuff the objects she had prepared inside the small fleece satchel she had found. She completely disregarded the burning aroma entering through the window, as it was strangely familiar to her by then. Whenever Abaven was excited, he would breath fire. Holding it in meant steam would pour from his nose, which resulted in the smokey smell that hung in the air.

Meanwhile, her dragon lay curled in a ball, casting an eye toward the window high above him.

Normally, he would gaze at the tower wondering what his princess could be doing. But today he knew.

Just like Celestia, Abaven had waited and wished every day for her father (or one of his messengers) to return and bring Celestia back to her kingdom. But now he knew that they might never return, and waiting for happiness would only cause Celestia more grief.

Today he had realized that Celestia would never be content, nor happy, in the confined tower that she had grown up in. She needed more than just four walls and a dragon to talk to; she needed to *live*.

Celestia peeked her head out of the tower, staring beyond her room, not a single ray of doubt visible in her features. Abaven immediately perked up at the sight of the princess and quickly moved beneath the window, staring up at her as she came to a stand on the window sill. She wore thick, black trousers and a satchel was slung across her shoulder, bulging and coming undone at the seams, containing everything she had prepared for the journey ahead of them.

When Abaven had first set his gaze on her short, unruly hair the day before, he was shocked.

He was so familiar with her long, lovely locks, it was hard for him to accept the change. But seeing her now, strands of gold cascading gently over her face, she seemed so fearless and self-assured. Her shorter locks of hair brought out a new side of her, and he was beginning to get used to it.

Casting her glittering, blue eyes towards her beast, her lips pulled into an enchanting smile, full of hope and ready for freedom.

Celestia clenched her eyes shut, bending her knees slightly. Giving her dragon just enough time to acknowledge what she was about to do.

And without another sound, she pushed off the stone and found herself midair, spiraling toward the ground. It seemed as though she lost her stomach and she found herself unable to keep her eyes open. Hopefully, she wasn't plunging to her death.

She stopped falling and opened her eyes, only to find herself atop her black and scaly beast. She made it!

Wrapping her arms tightly around him, she stared ahead, ignoring the scrapes she received with each turn and bend of flight.

With a powerful flap of his wings, the dragon rose in altitude, towering over the trees and brushing past clouds. There was so much more to see than she could remember from her first flight on Abaven's back. This time, there were no cuts or bruises to distract her from the beauty of the world surrounding her.

As she gazed beneath her she took immediate notice of the mini meadows and tiny trees. Everything was lush and green, easily pulling her gaze from one landmark to the next. Glittering rivers of crystal branched off into streams that flowed serenely through patches of saplings and shrubs. Abaven flew between jagged mountain tops that spiked up from the ground below, piercing the clouds that drifted by her.

She even caught glimpses of what she assumed were teeny tiny farms and villages scattered throughout the dense, expanding forest. Although she was too high to see any people, she imagined the little men and women tending to their gardens and playing with their children.

As hills and waterfalls, cliffs and lakes whooshed by, she felt as though she could finally find her place in that world.

All because she had finally taken the leap.

Chapter 6

Exhausted and hungry, Abaven finally located a clearing big enough for him to fit in. Upon landing, Celestia slid off Abaven's back and onto the grass below. He gazed down at her, smiling the best a dragon can, his fangs sticking out and scales shifting in odd directions.

He realized then, watching her twirl around the clearing, that she was no longer a little girl, reading fairy tales and wishing upon stars, or following him around the meadow and holding his tail. She had grown into a courageous young woman who wanted control over her own life, and had entrusted him to be a part of that life. When making her plans to escape the tower and find the meaning and purpose to her life, she had always included him in them. Even though he knew she was fully capable of fending for herself, Abaven would do his best to help and protect her along the way.

Abaven's thoughts disintegrated as his stomach began to rumble. Setting himself back on track, he studied the clearing, his nostrils dilating as he sniffed the air.

"You hungry, Abaven?" Celestia inquired. When Abaven nodded, both of their thoughts were brought back to the first time they had tried hunting. Although they hadn't planned to leave the tower until recently, Abaven had always found it important to teach Celestia key survival skills in case, one day, she would have to brave the world without him.

'Listen, Celestia. If you strain your ears, you might be able to hear leaves crunching. That usually means there is an animal nearby.' Abaven's head was swinging as he examined his surroundings, listening for even the slightest sound in the dense forest. He crouched against the forest floor and wagged his tail with anticipation. His eyes swept the area in search of prey. A small, barely audible crackle of leaves sounded deep within the forest. Looking beside him, he found Celestia gazing back at him with wide eyes.

'Did you hear that sound? Where did it come from?' Celestia pointed a tiny finger to her right.

Abaven nodded, and as he crept forward Celestia followed behind him. Spotting a large break in the trees, he gently lowered himself in, folding his wings back to slip through the tight opening. Gracefully twisting, turning, and landing, he settled his head between two trees. Celestia ran up beside him, exclaiming "Look!" She had caught sight of a deer, grazing in a clearing ahead of them. Abaven praised Celestia for her discovery and proudly nuzzled her with his snout.

Although he knew it was important that she learned how to catch and kill their prey, he figured then that Celestia was too young to watch the gruesome act. He directed her to close her eyes while he snatched a buck between his teeth. It struggled, trying to break free from the monster's jaws and refusing to give up. Abaven felt a pang in his heart for the creature, but he knew that sacrifice was necessary for survival. With a soft crunch, the animal fell motionless, no more struggles. No more breaths. No more movement.

Retracting his head from the bushes, he allowed Celestia to open her eyes and then ordered her to grab his tail so he could lead her safely back to the tower.

Upon reaching the meadow surrounding the tower, Abaven stopped and glanced back at Celestia, checking to make sure she was still gripping his tail. Celestia grinned up at him, and Abaven's scales shifted into an awkward smile as he let the carcass drop from his jaws.

Making sure that Celestia was paying attention, he inserted his claws into the mud and began shifting the pieces of dirt with his forehand and into a pile beside him. In mere seconds he dug a shallow hole. He found a log on the forest floor he gripped it between his teeth and shifted it over to the hole, dropping it in and allowing a spark of fire to latch onto it; he watched as it burnt and crackled within the hole with satisfaction.

He pushed the deer near the fire, sitting and waiting for it to heat up and become edible for the princess, but nothing happened. Celestia approached him, laughing, "you have to skin the creature before cooking it!" The dragon seemed to snort at his own mistake, puffs of smoke rising from his mouth as he attempted to skin the animal, but only ended up staining his claws in blood. "Can I give it a try, Abaven?" Celestia reasoned, cringing as Abaven accidentally ripped the wretched creature in half. Celestia groaned, pushing his claws away and motioning for him to sit down. He did so without much hesitation, silently retreating to a patch of grass and lying down, watching the princess with interest.

She made her way towards the deer with a rock and began carefully cutting off chunks of fur. Back when she had first lived in the castle, Celestia would often help the servants and had spent several hours of her time observing them prepare meals. From dicing potatoes to skinning deer, Celestia had seen it all. And although they hadn't let her do it herself very often, Celestia had easily picked up on their methods to prepare meals.

Abaven watched as Celestia carefully cut off the last few pieces of deerskin and then pierced the meat with a stick. She held the meat over the fire, patiently waiting for the flesh to turn gold.

Abaven and Celestia broke into a fit of laughter and smiles. Back then, he had tried to do everything for her and, in the end, she always ended up cleaning his mess.

Now, watching as Celestia easily tended to their dinner and cooked the buck he had caught, Abaven realized just how far they had come. They had experienced and learned so many things together and had learned to understand each other.

They were a team, not because they worked so well together, but because they respected and cared for each other.

Chapter 7

The prince stumbled through the forest, the horse beneath him panting and whining, tired to the point of collapsing. But the prince forced his steed onward, gently kicking the horse's side and urging him forward. Even so, the horse grew more and more exhausted. Eventually, the animal planted its feet on the ground, refusing to move. The prince continued digging his heels into the horse's side, but the animal didn't budge. With an angry snort, the horse rose high on its hind legs, sending the prince tumbling to the ground beneath him as it bolted into the forest.

The prince's arm twisted behind him, forcing him to let out a pained scream. But the agony was only temporary, fading after just a few minutes.

The prince's eyes trailed helplessly after the horse as it trotted away. He quickly pushed himself to his feet, running after his steed. But the horse was too fast, and the prince soon found himself toppling over from exhaustion. Sweat beaded his forehead and long, strained breaths escaped from his mouth. He swiped his blonde locks out of his eyes and whipped around. How was he supposed to continue his journey when his supplies and transportation had literally run away from him? The prince felt immediately like giving up, but something stopped him from doing so. Maybe it was his pride. Or his fear of seemingly enchanted forests. Or the fact it wasn't uncommon for him to have bad luck... as things like this happened all the time. But he had no idea.

The prince continued to stumble through the stand of trees lining the pathway. He could barely see past their thick trunks, and beyond that the forest seemed to close in on itself. Mysterious creaking and scratching noises seemed to surround him, making him feel as though he was trapped. His eyes restlessly skimmed over every detail of the woods encasing him. Although every step was hesitant and shaky, he knew his only hope was to stumble onward. He had to trudge over the layers of dried leaves and tree roots, past the mysterious rattling bushes and hissing leaves. And stumble onward he did.

Just when he felt he couldn't take another step forward, he smelt a faint waft of smoke. Confused, he took another couple of steps forward, the pungent smell of smoke strengthening. Maybe he wasn't lost after all, the smoke had to mean civilization! The prince's heart swelled with hope; no more darkness and scary woods for him! He quickened his pace, smiling as the scent grew stronger, strong enough, in fact, that he soon began coughing and his vision was clouding with grey smoke.

How would he find civilization if he couldn't see it? As if answering his own question, he held his breath and shielded his eyes. He stepped forward cautiously and took five small steps before a smile tugged at his lips and he continued onward with confidence. Almost immediately, he crashed into the rough bark of a large tree trunk. Brilliant planning, he thought, a huff escaping his lips.

Landing on his rump with an "oof", he rubbed his eyes, forgetting to shield them but quickly finding that the smoke had cleared. He could still *smell* it, but the thick cloud of smoke had completely dissipated. With triumph, he lifted himself from the ground, jogging onward with hope... Which soon melted as he began to tire once more. The adrenaline had drained from his system and he was, most definitely, much weaker due to the blistering hot sun and dense air. Or at least that's what he told himself.

Panting from exhaustion, he toppled over, landing in a heap on the ground. As he fought to catch his breath he recognized the feeling of grass beneath his fingertips. He lifted his gaze and took in the view; a grassy meadow dotted with wildflowers. He was intensely grateful he had found something other than a rough tree trunk to look at. Casting his gaze upward he noticed a thick trail of smoke rising into the air and followed it back down to its owner, a giant black dragon camouflaged within the shadows. The dragon's eyes were closed.

The prince rubbed his eyes. The only reason he could tell he wasn't dreaming was the sight and smell of the smoke emitting from the dragon's snout. Unsheathing his sword, the prince stepped slowly toward the dragon, eyeing its draped wing suspiciously. He had never felt braver.

He stepped cautiously, muffling his footsteps by avoiding twigs and leaves. Carefully walking around the dragon, he spotted a gap between its tail and its wing and peered inside, but the shadows made it nearly impossible to see. Slowly moving forward and straining to see, he was careful not to touch the beast for fear of awakening it. Just then, a gentle ray of sunlight fell across the face of a young woman, curled up on the ground within the protective circle of the dragon's wings.

Suddenly, the dragon shifted slightly and the prince tensed, pulling away and stumbling several steps backward. The beast was holding this girl captive. He had to save her! With sweaty palms, he tightened the grip on his sword, aiming it at the sleeping beast's back and charging forward. In the heat of the moment, he let out a blood-curdling battle cry, startling both the beast and the sleeping princess awake.

Celestia instantly jumped into action, swinging herself over the beast's tail and putting herself between the dragon and the charging prince. She spread her arms wide, as though creating a barrier between the mythical and the real. Her eyes blazed as they met those of the prince, who immediately skidded to a stop mere feet away from the princess. His sword was only inches from her nose. As the prince studied her features, he shrank back, feeling immediately intimidated.

"Step away." Celestia growled, her voice deep and hushed. *Nobody* harmed the dragon. The prince obeyed, scared out of his wits, and confused at the same time, he had only charged in order to save the girl! The dragon towered over the two of them, watching intently. His eyes never left those of the prince. Celestia turned back to gaze at the beast, who lowered his head and allowed her to pet his snout. The prince, seeing he had completely misjudged the entire situation, lowered his sword and dropped his head in confusion.

"I thought you were in trouble-" began the Prince. Celestia blocked out his voice, studying him and trying to determine whether or not he was a threat.

"Look at me." She ordered, and he did as told. Upon meeting his gaze, Celestia felt the slightest tug of memory. She was immediately puzzled by the familiarity of his jade-colored eyes. Overwhelmed by a nostalgic feeling of confusion and abandonment, Celestia quickly dropped her gaze, turning away from the prince and shooing him with her hand.

"Leave." She commanded. Celestia had such an intimidating figure and demanding presence that the prince found himself unable to speak. He opened his mouth to protest, but seeing the dragon glowering at him, he turned to go.

He turned to walk back toward the woods, hesitating briefly to look over his shoulder.

"I could've really used your help." Celestia's head snapped up in confusion at his words, and with that last whisper, he disappeared into the growing shadows of the forest.

Celestia slowly shook her head, coming to the realization that there were people out there who wouldn't hesitate to kill her dragon. To others, Abaven was nothing more than a big hulking monster.

Although she worried for her dragon, her mind still buzzed with the prince's parting words. What did he mean, how could he have used her help? She had barely been out in the real world for less than a day! How could she possibly help anyone? The more she tried to answer her questions, the more befuddled she became.

Exhaustion soon overtook her and she pushed aside her confusion, laying down in the grass and brushing the lingering questions from her mind as sleep tugged at her consciousness. And so, ignoring the previous events, she allowed herself to drift asleep. Her beast circled around her and once more draped his wing over their figures. The scene of her surging forward, rushing to protect him from the charging prince, continued to play in Abaven's mind. She hadn't so much as hesitated to protect him; she truly cared for the beast more than herself.

Chapter 8

Celestia jolted awake, sweat droplets trickling down her forehead and her hands tugging at the grass beneath her. Glimpses of a burning castle and thick, choking smoke flashed in and out of her mind. She could still faintly hear the screams and pleas, but she couldn't recall where those thoughts were coming from. She struggled to push the endless, torturous memories away, her breath rigid and her throat tightening.

Celestia's sudden movements caused the beast to stir. His eyes snapped open and he lowered his head beside her, shifting his body and causing Celestia to notice his presence.

"Sorry for waking you." She breathed. Her eyes clenched shut as tears dribbled down her cheeks. The beast nuzzled his snout into her side. She knew, without a shadow of a doubt, that he cared. That he understood her words and her pain, and that he had always cared. This thought comforted her and it strengthened her.

Celestia's hands shakily wrapped around his snout. She snuggled against it, her grip tightening around it as though it was her lifeline. At the moment, it may have been.

When the tears finally began to slow and her silent sobs shortened, she slid from his snout and back onto the ground. She rubbed her eyes quickly, silencing her heart's cries for help. As she stood on shaky legs she mustered all the strength she could and clenched her hands by her sides. She would not shrink under the power of her thoughts. She would conquer them. Soul set ablaze, she turned to look the beast in the eye.

Her eyes glittered with a sense of hope she had lost only days before, something she hadn't had for a long time. He could feel her true self coming back. Slowly but steadily.

Celestia walked over his tail, stepping out of her circle of protection and into the world of danger outside. The cool morning air bit at her skin and the wind whipped through her hair. But she liked it, she felt free. And she smiled. She smiled because she was there and because she had hope. She had a dragon, a companion, a friend. And that, at the moment, it was all she needed.

She allowed the sun's rays to caress her face and stood there for a few seconds before turning back to her beast. He sat upright, resting his gaze on her and observing her movements. The girl who was crying only moments ago had changed in a matter of seconds.

As she had turned toward the beast, she had caught a glimpse of black glittering between his scales. Her eyes softened and she walked over to him, motioning for him to lower his head, which he did without protest. Celestia studied his figure, immediately noticing the scrapes and wounds he had suffered over the past few days. Peculiarly, she had ached in the same spots where each of his wounds was visible.

She reached into her satchel, pulling out one of the spare blouses she had sewn. She carefully ripped a large piece of fabric from the bottom and, popping the cork from the top of her waterskin, she dribbled cool, clear water over the fabric and soaked it through. She used the wet fabric to wipe the black liquid from the dragon's scales, gently cleaning in between each one. The dried pieces fell to the ground, the dragon wincing with each scrape. Celestia softened her grip on the rag and cleaned the wound on his snout, petting him to calm his constant whines or growls of disapproval. She moved to the wound on his leg and proceeded to clean it, too.

When finished, she stepped away from the beast as he stretched out, relieved his scales were no longer stuck in clusters and itching his skin.

As the sun began to rise, Celestia figured it was time for departure. After the incident with the prince, who had attempted to stab her dragon, Celestia realized that they could easily encounter violent villagers if they flew too close to the trees; Abaven could be struck by arrows or hit with rocks. On the contrary, flying too high for long amounts of time made Celestia nauseous and dizzy, and so that couldn't be an option either.

"I think I'll have to travel by foot while you fly up above- it would be safest for the both of us," she concluded. Abaven growled worriedly, 'But what if you're in danger and you need me? How will we meet at the end of the day?'

Celestia reached into her satchel and pulled out her dagger.

"I can protect myself, Abaven! I promise I'll be fine. And at the end of the day, you can meet me in one of the clearings up ahead." She reassured him, but Abaven peered at her hesitantly. Celestia sighed, thinking of a way she could call to her beast if she found shelter or needed his aid.

"If I am in danger or have stopped to rest for the evening, I will simply whistle," she concluded, letting out a long and sharp whistle in a demonstration. Although Abaven did not like the idea of her wandering alone, he nodded his head in agreement. Once her mind was set, there was no changing it.

Celestia then started toward the forest, her beast hot on her trail. As she stopped where the grass met trees, she turned back toward the dragon behind her.

"Goodbye, Abaven" Celestia whispered, kissing his snout in parting. He whimpered his own goodbye. He knew they would only part for a short while, and though he wished he could travel on foot with her, the trees had grown too dense and he could not walk through them.

Abaven wistfully watched as Celestia turned, smiling reassuringly back at him as she disappeared into the dark forest. He watched after her a few more moments before taking off, spiraling toward the clouds and straining his vision in order to see Celestia through the tops of trees.

Celestia's feet danced across the dirt, avoiding twisting branches slashing the air, and tree roots wiggling through the mud. The thick roof of leaves above her did not stop rain from dripping onto her head. It wasn't until she first shivered that Celestia realized for the first time in her life, as far as she could remember, she was on her own. With every step further into the dreary forest, she felt more radiant and free. As the rain cleansed her hair and dampened her cloak, she twirled gracefully along the path, droplets running off her form with each rotation of her feet. She felt *alive*.

Then she heard something like a creak, a crunch, or a whisper. Her ears perked up and she stopped dead in her tracks, staring ahead of her cautiously. In just a second, she had gone from feeling liberated and eager to feeling jittery and alert.

The bushes beside her rustled and she spun toward them, glaring them down with such intensity it could kill. That is, if looks could kill.

She gripped the dagger in her satchel anxiously, nearing the bushes and bringing it slowly above her head. Just as she was about to impale the bushes with her knife, the prince's head protruded from the bushes and he screamed "PLEASE DON'T HURT ME!"

Startled, Celestia jumped back, watching him warily as he tumbled out of the shrubbery and landed face first in the mud beside her. She backed up, bitterly focusing on the man who had not only tried to harm her dragon but was apparently following her as well. He slowly pushed himself back onto his feet and hastily wiped mud out of his eyes. Their eyes met and, again, a weird feeling of reminiscence overcame Celestia. She quickly pulled away her gaze and, instead of feeling somber, allowed herself to be overcome with irritation.

"You followed me." Celestia acknowledged. His gaze dropped to his feet, immediately flustered.

"Well... not exactly.." He fumbled with his hands. Celestia glared at him, then turned on her heel and continued down the trail.

"Wait!" the prince called.

Celestia sped up, exhaling with agitation as he caught up and trudged beside her. They remained silent for a matter of time, Celestia hoping he would just disappear. In truth, she wished the prince would leave her be. For the first time in her life, she was on her own and able to make decisions for herself, but suddenly this prince was encroaching on her freedom and space.

Unfortunately, her hopes failed her, and he stayed glued to her side.

"Leave." Celestia growled once more, the prince flinched, but decidedly stayed put. He immediately added that to his list of brave acts... which was a very short list.

"I j-j-just t-thought... we could h-help each other! I c-could help you get wherever... you're heading. And you could m-maybe he-help me find my horse? I lost it y-y-yesterday and you j-just seemed ki-kind of good with animals." The prince trembled, a true man with words. Celestia gazed at him from the corner of her eye.

"Fine, I will help you," She grumbled, ignoring his ridiculous grin of triumph. She wouldn't admit it, but with him beside her, Celestia no longer feared the woods around her. In addition, no matter how desperately she wished to be alone, Celestia's heart refused to allow her to turn him away. There was something too familiar about him, something she couldn't quite assess.

"Where do you plan on going? My navigating skills are pretty precise."

Celestia didn't have an answer, she didn't know where she was going. To her, the journey mattered far more than the destination.

Chapter 9

Celestia quickly learned that the prince detested silence. As soon as their conversation would come to a halt, he urgently spouted out whatever was on the top of his head. It wasn't long until he asked "I don't believe I know your name. What shall I call you?" Celestia debated on whether or not she should tell him her name. Could he use it against her in the future? Figuring it was quite useless to dispute, she shrugged her shoulders.

"I call myself Celestia."

The prince nodded, as though struggling to recall the name while he coughed out his own.

"I'm Maverick." Maverick wanted to add something like 'The Great And Powerful' or 'The Bravest Prince Ever' to the end of his name (to make it sound more interesting) but realized Celestia would probably desert him if he did. Luckily, she just nodded her head in response to his name, avoiding his eyes and absorbing the silence. The only sound to be heard was the tramping of their feet and the wind whistling through the leaves.

"You're her aren't you?" Maverick questioned, throwing Celestia a side glance. But her facial expression only shifted slightly, showing her change of thought in the smallest of ways. A mere quirk of her eyebrow.

"It depends who you're talking of," replied Celestia.

Maverick scoffed, but continued on anyway. "The lost princess... A mere folk tale until now!"

Celestia stopped walking to glare at Maverick. He skidded to a stop in front of her, turning to gaze back at her malicious expression. What had he done wrong?

"I am not from a fairytale, nor was I ever. I was not lost, I was forgotten. There is a difference." And with that, she sent him one more challenging glare before quickening her pace. Maverick slowly turned to catch up with her, puzzled by her rapidly alternating behaviors.

Seeing Celestia had been infuriated with his reference to her as "the lost princess", he decided that maybe he should take a step back and find a way to earn her trust. He decided to talk about his life as a Prince, which was his favorite thing to talk about.

Maverick continued talking for seemingly hours as they walked on, taking small breaths to lick his chapping lips, blow hair from his face, or stop altogether and catch a breath. He described the palace where he lived, his family, his friends, the people who served in the palace and the many duties and obligations of being a prince. Every once in a while, Celestia would interrupt his jabbering to ask a question or make a comment, but she mostly kept her thoughts to herself. She listened intently, learning things she had never even thought of before.

"...We have banquets every now and then, where we eat and dance until the sun rises..." Maverick blabbered on.

"...Ever since I was eight years old I have been taught and trained to ride a horse, along with my other studies. Horses are fairly friendly creatures... that is... if they like you. I have had a certain horse, Star, for years... but she seems to have run away..."

"That's terrible." Celestia spoke, her voice dropping to show her concern, but she quickly piped up. Although Celestia found Maverick persistent and annoying, she found herself becoming relaxed around him. He filled the uneasy stillness of the forest with a constant blabber, and it made Celestia feel secure.

"I haven't seen a horse up close in a fairly long time, are they as majestic as they seem from afar?"

Maverick nodded, smiling at the subject.

"They have the longest, most beautiful mane of hair. Their mane is soft to the touch, as well as their coats. When you ride on a horse for the first time you feel as though you're above all else, it gives you a sense of wonder and fear all at once..." Celestia found it curious how each of his words reminded her of her dragon.

"Well then, I suppose your horse and my dragon are quite alike! My dragon has dazzling, transcendent scales and, although they aren't soft, they're smooth upon contact. And when I first flew with him, I was exhilarated and anxious all at once!" She relayed, and Maverick looked at her wildly.

"Well... I think they're a little bit different..."

"Don't be scared of Abaven, he's the most benevolent beast you'll ever come across."

"I reckon you're very attached to your dragon?"

"Well, of course. He's all I've got- he's been watching over me since I was little. In truth, he's my only friend." Suddenly, Celestia realized to what extent she missed Abaven, and awaited their reunion.

Maverick smiled dolefully, pondering how challenging Celestia's life must have been. He couldn't help but conjecture what it would feel like to be trapped in a tower with nobody to speak to except a dragon.

Finally, they came to a clearing in the woods and Celestia shushed Maverick, whistling. She feared for a moment that he wouldn't hear her, but heard a low roar echo in response and felt immediate comfort. Maverick looked at her questioningly.

"Just wait." she ordered, slowly sinking to the ground in the middle of the field. The prince stood idly beside her, observing the field and following her movements with his gaze.

Dozens of pure white daisies fluttered in the dying breeze, swaying to and fro. Celestia picked a few from the blades of grass, separating them from their beds and placing them in her hair. She loved their soft, silky texture and bright, showy colors.

The daisies she had been collecting flew from her hand, causing her to gaze upwards. There was a whirring sound, much like the wind rustling through the trees.

Two large, black wings lowered her dragon into the clearing, the blades of grass waving hello to Abaven. His claws dug into the ground as he landed next to the two figures.

Celestia leapt from her place among the flowers and dashed towards Abaven, her heavily draped clothes barely slowing her with the sudden burst of energy she felt.

She wrapped her fragile arms around one of her beast's scaly legs. He lowered his head, nuzzling the princess with his snout before setting himself down. Celestia, climbing between his outstretched wings and long neck, nuzzled into the grass beside him. It was then that Abaven perceived Maverick and began growling, but Celestia quickly hushed him.

"That's Maverick, he means no harm. He just needs some help finding his lost horse," she reassured him. Abaven rolled his eyes, but knew that if Celestia put her trust in the scrawny little prince, then he should too.

Meanwhile, the prince stared at the two in astonishment. How had Celestia taught her beast to return to her at the sound of a whistle? Why hadn't he thought of teaching his horse that trick?! If only he could whistle and Star would come back to find him.

But then again, there was clearly an extraordinary bond between Celestia and her dragon, one nobody could possibly understand except them. It was obvious that they could communicate in many distinctive ways.

Although Maverick could have puzzled over the companionship of Celestia and Abaven for hours, he came to a sudden realization that the sun was quickly fading and the night air was becoming decidedly cold. He turned away from the princess and her beast, beginning to gather sticks and placing them in a small pile beside him. He then backed away a safe distance, looking into the dragon's fading eyes in silent plea. The dragon snorted, sending a tiny spark toward the bundled sticks and contentedly watching as it caught fire immediately.

Abaven settled in for the evening, Celestia curling up beside his warm chest as he draped his wings over the both of them. He kept his left eye open, despite his fatigue, and it fixed on the prince, who was warming himself by the fire and eating a piece of stale bread... which he had found in his pocket. He watched Maverick for a little while, fascinated by his awkward movements. Every action was jittery, less poised than those of Celestia.

Although Abaven found the presence of another human strange, and desired to observe him further, exhaustion overtook the beast and soon he, too, slumbered.

Chapter 10

Celestia awoke to Maverick shaking her and whispering fervently, "I'm absolutely starving, Celestia! I debated letting you sleep in, but I don't have any weapons to hunt with... and I'm not quite sure which berries and nuts are edible. Can you please help me?"

Celestia rolled her eyes, quietly arising, careful not to awake Abaven. She petted his arm in parting and then grabbed her satchel, reaching in and pulling out her dagger.

"Follow me," she nodded, and Maverick absently drifted along behind her. Celestia smiled as she breathed in the crisp, minty morning air that left her feeling refreshed. She gently ordered Maverick to pick a bunch of fluorescent pink berries while she hounded a couple of rabbits they could eat for breakfast.

Finally, five dead rabbits and one pound of berries later, Celestia and Maverick returned to the campsite. Abaven awoke upon their arrival, his yellow eyes fixing on the food they carried in their arms. He immediately perked up, obviously quite hungry as well.

Celestia and Maverick began the process of preparing two rabbits for supper and, as for the other three rabbits, the beast got those. He gulped them down fur and all, in the blink of an eye.

After skinning the rabbits and slathering berry juice over their flesh, Celestia set off to find the firewood.

While her feet crunched fallen brown leaves and the wind caressed her face, she began to hum to herself. Celestia dug through leaves and small twigs, fetching the larger pieces of wood that hid beneath the blanket of debris. Looking around, she recognized the environment around her. She had met Abaven in this area of the woods over a decade ago. It was in these woods that she had learned her dragon's name and they had first become acquainted. Even though she was just a child, it was here that she had come to know Abaven as her protector.

As two of the palace servants, Ulric and Fendrel, helped Celestia step out of the carriage, she took immediate notice of the thick trees looming around her. Where was *she*?

"Don't worry, Celestia," Fendrel reassured her, noticing the troubled look on her face. He smiled down at her and grabbed her small hand in his own.

"Abaven will be here any minute and he will take you the rest of the way to the tower."

Before Celestia even had the chance to ask who Abaven was, or why she was going to a tower, a small creature dropped in through a gap in the treetops. It landed clumsily in front of her, falling over in a dusty cloud of dirt. It shook the grime from its scales, shifting its gaze towards Celestia as its mouth shifted into what she assumed was a toothy smile. A small spout of steam arose from its snout and it leapt towards Celestia in excitement. Based on the creatures glistening black scales, razor-sharp claws, and large leathery wings, Celestia knew immediately that the critter in front of her was a dragon. A baby dragon.

Bouncing forward, the dragon earnestly licked her face and caused her to giggle. Although it was nearly triple her size, the dragon wasn't nearly as frightening as she had imagined one would be!

"This is Abaven," Ulric said laughingly, pushing him gently away from Celestia.

"He'll be leading you the rest of the way to your destination. We wish we could accompany you, but we have to follow your father's orders. In terms of your protection, it is best that we leave as quickly as possible."

Ulric and Fendril both gave the tiny princess Celestia an encouraging hug before quickly clambering into the carriage. Celestia called after them "Why can't you come with me?" but they didn't hear her. She smiled sadly, waving goodbye to the palace servants as they disappeared hastily into the forest.

After staring after the carriage for a long while, Celestia felt a tug on her dress. She turned to face the dragon, who motioned with a flick of his head for her to follow him. She stumbled after him, grabbing a hold of his tail so that she wouldn't get left behind.

"Your name is Abaven?" She inquired, wondering why the dragon had such a strange name. He turned his head slightly, looking back at her.

'Yes, I'm Abaven. Your father gave me this name to ensure you knew why I was here. He told me it means protector in an olden language his ancestors used to use, and I am here to protect you, Celestia.'

Celestia looked at the dragon, baffled. His response had come in a series of thoughts and, although reasonably it could have been all in her head, she somehow knew it was him. She could talk to Abaven! Since she had a few questions she had never gotten the chance to ask the servants, she decided to ask Abaven instead.

"Why do I need protecting?" She inquired, wobbling over roots and rocks as she followed behind him.

'Your father told me that there are dangerous things in this world that could harm you, Celestia. He said the only place you're safe is the tower I'm taking you to.'

Celestia shivered, her eyes flashing all around her.

"What kind of things?"

'I'm not quite sure. Just know that no matter what happens, I will be here and I will do everything in my power to keep you safe. From this point on, Celestia, I am your Abaven.'

Celestia snapped from her daze and realized Maverick had been calling for her, she had been gone far too long.

She quickly gathered the sticks and branches in her arms and walked silently back toward the clearing. As soon as she set the firewood down in the pit they had dug, her beast lit the wood aflame. The fire immediately began to dance as the flames grew and sparked in the late afternoon air.

After impaling the meat on a stick and wedging it in place over the flames, Celestia left the rest of the dinner preparations to Maverick and went to talk to her dragon.

"Do you remember this segment of the forest?" Abaven answered with a grin and nod of his head. Celestia beamed up at him.

"We've come so far, since then, and yet you have never once failed to be my protector. Thank you, Abaven." She stated, petting his snout gently. She knew that she would have never gotten this far without him. Abaven hummed as if to say, 'I will always be here if you need me.'

Maverick, oblivious to the intimate conversation occuring between the girl and her beast, yelped "Breakfast is ready!"

Celestia turned and ran back to Maverick. The meat had turned a crispy rose gold color, a savory aroma emitting from it. Celestia withdrew her rabbit and held it in the chilling air to cool off. After a few moments, she took hold of both ends of the stick and bit into the juicy meat, relishing each delicious bite and not caring at all that grease was dribbling down her chin.

Maverick studied her grease stained fingers and oily lips, wondering why she ate the meat straight from the stick. Celestia took notice and beckoned him to join in.

"You'll not find fancy china plates and silver cutlery here, Prince." she said laughingly. "You'll enjoy our delicious feast more while it's still hot."

Maverick sat still for a moment, processing Celestia's words, then took a small bite from the tender meat. He immediately forgot his manners, tearing at the flesh and swallowing mouthfuls at a time.

Finally, they had finished their meal and the sun was nearly at its highest point in the sky. Celestia and Maverick headed off into the woods once more, Abaven flying over the treetops and worrying little of Celestia's well being. She'd be fine!

With full stomachs, Celestia and Maverick were able to push through the tree thicket promptly. They increased speed, hoping to reach a suitable destination where they could safely spend another night.

Suddenly, at the edge of the woods, they came to a river running with clear water. Celestia cautiously stepped to the edge of the river, knelt down and scooped a handful of water, drinking from her hands. Maverick grabbed her by the arm and pulled her from the river's edge, causing her to spill her hands' contents.

"Careful." He cautioned, motioning toward the rapidly flowing water. "The current is much too strong here. If you were to fall in, you would be swept downstream. Let's find somewhere a little less dangerous to quench our thirst once we cross to the other side."

Maverick moved further up the riverbank, looking for a safer path and suddenly saw where the trail on the other side of the river began. There seemed to be a walkway of stones leading from this side of the river across to the trail on the other side. He motioned to Celestia to follow his movements.

He began to hop from stone to stone above the water's strengthening current. Celestia followed along after Maverick, struggling to maintain the same footing patterns. Jumping to the last rock, Maverick held out a hand to Celestia, but she leapt toward the shore, ignoring his outstretched hand. She could brave it on her own.

Her foot slipped on the rock's uneven surface and she fell into the freezing water. The cold was immediate and intense, needle-like pains engulfing her body to the extent she could barely breathe. She could feel herself slipping away with the current, the cold sapping her strength and her only thought was that if she didn't drown she would surely freeze to death.

Maverick's eyes frantically searched the river for her, but she was gone.

Chapter 11

Everything was black. Her body was numb, her limbs ached, and her lungs were bursting with the need for air. Celestia's head occasionally broke through the water's surface as she thrashed in the currents, but all she received with each attempt was another mouthful of freezing water.

Her legs scraped against rocks and her body was bashed from side to side, leaving a trail of blood following after her as she thrashed through the river. The current pulled her under and her vision clouded over as she attempted to catch a breath. She struggled against the powerful river but felt herself quickly weakening, leaving her lungs to fill with water as she floated nearly lifelessly down the river. Even Abaven, she thought, couldn't save her.

Maverick thundered through the forest alongside the river's edge. He struggled to whistle for the beast to help him as he tripped over roots and his legs sunk knee deep in thick, oozing mud. But his efforts seemed to be in vain, his breaths too shaky and uncertain. He knew that Celestia's safety was in his hands and he was determined to come to her rescue.

He scrambled forward, mud sucking at his boots and striving to halt his attempts. He knew time was running out and, with a final burst of strength, freed himself from the oozing mud. Adrenaline coursed through his veins as he raced alongside the river. He spotted Celestia's grey cloak surfacing in the raging water, which only made him move faster.

The world seemed determined to slow him down, trees throwing their twisted branches in his way. But alas, he managed to break through most of them, searching the river for another glimpse of the endangered princess. Jagged limbs tore his clothes and scratched his face, leaving cuts and streaks of blood that he didn't even seem to notice. The pain might have slowed him down, but he wouldn't allow it.

As he neared a curving stretch between one side of the forest and another, he managed to see Celestia's drowning body floating in the river. His feet thundered across the ground and he neared yet another obstacle between him and his destination.

Realizing that he would have to leap across a stream, he leant forward, accelerating faster and pushed off the edge of the bank with a great roar. Just as his feet had left the ground, he felt the river bank crumble beneath him. Instead of soaring over the water he tumbled face first into it. 'Really, Maverick?' he thought to himself. Thankfully, this part of the stream was calm, and he quickly hoisted himself to his feet and ran toward the princess.

Her body had washed up along a shallow pebble shore, stuck there despite the extremely powerful current trying to pull her back in. Maverick stumbled through the water to reach Celestia as quickly as possible. Rolling her over and dragging her from the river to the safety of the bank, he couldn't help but recoil in fear as he looked down at her.

Her eyes were open.

Maverick's first thought was that Celestia was dead. But even though her eyes seemed glazed over, she was breathing shallowly, so she couldn't have been dead. Maverick blinked, and when he looked at her once more, her eyes had closed. Rubbing his eyes, he blinked again. They remained closed. Declaring himself crazy, he knelt next to her and debated what to do. The situation completely cleared his mind of Celestia's open eyes and the fact this wouldn't have happened if she accepted his help.

Then Maverick remembered- when he was a child, if he accidentally inhaled water or choked on food his mother would pat him on the back until he coughed it up. Keeping this in mind, he quickly turned Celestia on her side, forcefully slapping her back until finally she began to spew out river water. Once she had coughed up enough water, he gently laid her on the ground. He ripped fabric from his shirt, dabbed it in the chilly river, and wiped at her wounds.

Maverick noticed that Celestia's lips seemed to be turning blue and suddenly realized that she was probably freezing after her ordeal in the river. Checking once again to make sure she was breathing, Maverick began to make a fire. He tried to whistle one more time to summon Celestia's beast, but he, too, was shivering with cold and could not purse his lips to make even the slightest sound. Grunting in annoyance, he gathered sticks and dried grasses and used two sharp stones from the riverbank, striking them together to produce a spark. Soon he had a roaring fire to dry and warm the two of them. He glanced back at her, noticing that her lips were no longer blue and that she seemed to be breathing more steadily. He could only hope that her injuries were minor, but he wouldn't really know until she stirred.

Celestia awoke to the flickering of firelight and a blanket of stars over her head. Startled, she pushed herself up, immediately light headed. Although it seemed like she had coughed up half the river when she had been tossed onto the pebbled shore, she still felt like she had swallowed the other half; her throat was scratchy and her head throbbed. Maverick eyed her with sympathy, but still awkwardly sat to the side, wondering if he should go to her aid, but remembering all the times she had brushed aside his attempts, including the final offer of help that had landed her in the river. He decided to let her fend for herself.

Celestia stood up, swaying slightly as she regained her balance. Her throat was scratchy, keeping her from uttering a single sound. She owed him thanks, but the words wouldn't pass her lips.

Maverick seemed to read her mind, uttering a nearly inaudible, "you're welcome."

She wondered why this practical acquaintance of hers, almost a stranger, had apparently risked his own life to save hers, judging from the scrapes and bruises on his face and arms. In fact, she didn't know why he still tagged along. But something kept her from shooing him away, and she couldn't quite tell just what it was. She felt this brave, extraordinary act could be her new reason to keep him around.

Maverick attempted to convince Celestia that she needed rest, but she ignored him, walking back towards the trail by the river. Maverick was quickly coming to realize that there was no changing her mind when it came to, well, anything. Even if all she needed was rest.

The only problem was, she had no idea which direction they had come from. Maverick slowly pushed himself up, his legs aching and sore. He didn't dare complain, as he knew Celestia's pain was probably excruciatingly greater than his own. He grabbed a stick and held it over the fire until it lit, walking to the right of the pebbled area and urging Celestia to follow him (as though he actually knew where he was going). Deciding to trust him, Celestia trailed him into the forest.

But as Celestia followed Maverick down the forest trail she began to feel concerned for the beast. Where was he? Was he looking for her, too? Had he felt her pain with her? Without thinking, she whistled for him, only to be cut off mid-whistle by Maverick's hand clamped over her mouth. She raised her eyebrows, licking his hand, which he retracted in disgust and silently wiped on his trousers.

"You never know who or what's out there... watching and listening." He whispered. Celestia rolled her eyes, but silently continued forward anyway. She was quickly coming to realize that there were many unseen dangers in the outside world, she had experienced them and seen them time and time before. She had even experienced a few of them herself, but those dangers were not enough to send her scurrying back to the safety of her tower.

Shivering at both the memory and the eerie feeling, Celestia longed for Abaven to be there beside her. She wished they didn't have to part ways and could brave the world side by side.

She also wished that they had given more thought into what they would do after leaving the tower. After all, she couldn't search through the woods her whole life and sleep in random clearings.

She longed for adventure.

Oh, if only at that moment she knew of the journey ahead of her.

Chapter 12

The bushes beside the two wanderers rustled, causing Maverick to jump back and shriek. After all his brave acts that night, he had officially gone back to the timid and fearful Maverick he usually was. Celestia, on the other hand, stared at the bushes silently. Her heart thundered against her ribs as she locked eyes with two, glowing orbs.

Although her mind was telling her to run (or shriek, like Maverick), she secretly wanted to see who that mesmerizing gaze belonged to. She ignored her instincts and slowly inched toward the trees. The eyes remained there, unblinkingly watching her. Her hand stretched toward them, but they closed, disappearing completely and leaving Celestia baffled.

She stood rooted to her spot, watching attentively for a matter of time, as though expecting the eyes to reappear. They did not; nothing but darkness remained in their place.

Maverick, waving the torch in front of him (just to be safe), walked to Celestia and urged her to continue searching for their former trail. Celestia sighed in disappointment, but nonetheless agreed. She knew they had to continue if they were ever to reach their destination, wherever that was.

The leaves next to them shifted again, rustling louder than before. Ignoring the sound, Celestia forced herself to speed up in order to keep pace with the prince. After all, he was the only one who actually knew where they were going. At least, she hoped he did.

Even though they ignored it, the sound seemed to follow them, bushes rustling with every step they took. Celestia thought she could see shadows of a creature illuminated in the torch-light and forced herself to continue moving forward, even though the cold, draining fear that pierced her heart was progressively harder to handle.

Suddenly, something jumped in front of them, facing them with those same, luminous eyes. Celestia gasped in awe as she gazed at the creature, a magnificent horse of pure white. It neighed softly, as though greeting the companions. Maverick yelped in astonishment, his eyes wide as he studied the horse.

"That's my lost horse! That's Star!" he cried in amazement.

Although this was the first time she could recall being face to face with such a mysterious mammal, she felt a wave of warmth, and found herself instantly drawn to the horse.

Celestia walked towards Star slowly, her right hand gently reaching towards the animal. 'Don't run' she thought, glancing back at Maverick from time to time. The horse trotted toward her, as if it had heard her thoughts, nuzzling its head into her hand and giving a small neigh of approval. Maverick joined the two joyfully, placing his hand on the Star's silky coat, only for the horse to stamp down on his foot with its heavy hooves. Maverick held in a yelp of pain and backed away from the horse to show his discomfort.

After several moments of marveling over their discovery, Celestia took a firm grip on the silky mane and instinctively pulled herself onto the horse's back, gripping the horse's reins in her hands. Star didn't budge, calm under the touch of Celestia. Sitting on Star felt almost as though she was atop Abaven, despite the fact her legs weren't being scraped by spiny scales. She stretched her hand to the prince, who folded his arms and shook his head.

"There is no way I'm getting back on that thing." The horse seemed to bob her head in agreement, but Celestia stretched her hand out anyway.

"We've got to get going and, based on what you've told me, horseback is faster. Can you two just try to get along for the rest of the journey? Is that too much to ask?" The prince nodded his head, glaring at Star in disapproval.

"Get on, or I'm leaving you here." Celestia stated, her patience thinning.

"Like you actually would." The prince huffed, but he took her hand anyway, vaulting onto the back of the horse. He knew she would.

Star turned and, without guidance, trotted in the direction they had been heading. The prince grabbed onto Celestia, fearing for his life; he nearly fell off with every trot. Celestia, being used to riding astride Abaven as he soared through the skies, found the bouncing and jolting of the horse a bit difficult, but she soon adjusted to the motion, and realized that the leather saddle was actually quite comfortable. She wondered if she could construct something similar for Abaven.

Although they were traveling much faster by horseback, Celestia knew traveling by dragonback would be much quicker. They could soar through the sky, swiftly reaching their destination before sunset. But she could never take the chance of Abaven being spotted by a villager, causing an uproar throughout the countryside. People would appear in mobs, bobbing pitchforks, firing arrows, and swinging swords in an attempt to harm her dragon. Celestia knew she could never gamble with Abaven's life so, for now, they would continue to travel by horseback. At least it was better than walking!

Her arms, however, began to ache with the unaccustomed exercise and her palms became sore from the rough leather reins which were tied in a loop. She realized that Star seemed to know exactly where it was going, so she dropped the reins, hugging the horse's neck instead.

Maverick grasped firmly onto Celestia's shoulders, his knuckles white and his teeth chattering.

Soon enough, they reached their former trail. The river disappeared behind them in seconds. Celestia was intensely grateful they had found

Maverick's lost horse (or that the horse had found them) otherwise, the journey would have taken much longer.

"How far is your kingdom from my tower?" The princess wondered aloud. How much longer would their journey take?

"Only a week or so of traveling horseback, rest-stops included." replied Maverick.

Celestia nodded and asked, "Can you see my tower from your kingdom?"

Maverick shook his head.

Celestia hesitated, hoping not to offend Maverick, then questioned, "Your life as royalty sounds pleasing to me, so why did you leave?"

Maverick seemed to choke on air, but nevertheless decided to respond. He had guessed the question would come eventually.

"My father... he was in an argument with the ruler of the Eastern kingdom, who had recently become an ally of ours. They were whispering, but loud enough that I could hear from the hallway. I overheard my father speak of keeping his daughter safe. Daughter? What daughter? As far as I knew I was an only child, so I had no idea what was going on.

"I was dazed, as you can imagine, and as soon as my father left the counseling room I pulled him aside. I confronted him on what I had heard, and he reluctantly told me the truth: I did indeed have a sister. She is just a few years older than me and had been taken somewhere deep in the forest when I was an infant. He said something about how it was for her safety, but I can't quite remember the rest."

Maverick nearly stopped talking, but felt the need to explain himself.

"After he had admitted the truth, he told me that the time wasn't right, that I couldn't see her. He told me it was too dangerous and instructed me not to pursue her. But, as much as I wanted to listen to my father, I knew that she was out there somewhere. She was out there alone and I needed to show her I exist. I needed to show her that someone cared enough to search for her; I've always wanted an older sister. I probably shouldn't have left without many provisions or guidance, without anything other than a horse and a satchel... but I couldn't wait..."

Celestia no longer heard the words that spilled from Maverick's mouth, retracting into her mind. Her thoughts whirred with images, flashing back to the day she had been taken from her kingdom and relocated to the tower. She could feel the tension in the air once more, hear the guilt in her parents' voices. She could feel her father tugging her away, but she looked back at her mother. Right before she turned, walking back into the castle, Celestia focused on the bundle of blankets her mother clutched something in her arms- what was it?

As Celestia strained her memory, shuffled through her thoughts, and searched through her mind, she realized that the bundle of blankets in her mother's arms contained a child. It was her brother, she had a younger brother.

Celestia's eyes widened, the gears in her head had finally clicked into place. Maverick's strikingly similar hair color and facial features, they were no longer just a coincidence. The deep sense of nostalgia and comfort she felt around Maverick suddenly made sense.

"I know who your sister is," Celestia managed to whisper, interrupting him. Maverick became silent, his eyes wild as he looked up at her. Celestia paused, as though she couldn't believe it herself.

"It's been awhile, brother."

Chapter 13

Celestia waited patiently for Star to begin grazing on berries, hoping she could pluck them and use them for breakfast. Since she wasn't familiar with the types of fruit in this region of the forest, she waited to see what berries Star deemed edible so she could gather some for Maverick and herself.

Finally, Star began gnawing on a clump of juicy black berries. Celestia picked a handful of the glistening, ripe berries and stuck them in a satchel dangling from the side of Star, which was already filled with things Maverick had smuggled from the kingdom before his departure. She lifted herself onto Star, who snatched another mouthful of the delicious berries before trotting back in the direction they had come from. The small tree thicket they had used as shelter was barely large enough to fit the three of them, let alone a dragon!

Celestia wondered if Abaven had found somewhere safe to rest. How was he holding up, was he as exhausted and sore as she was? She was concerned for his well-being, but trusted he was fine.

Over the years they were able to develop their ability to read each other's thoughts and anticipate each other's actions. Even though she was worried about the safety of her dragon, she felt as though if he were in trouble she'd know immediately. Taking deep breaths, Celestia was finally able to convince herself that her dragon was safe and sound. He was her dragon, after all, and he would not let harm fall upon himself if it meant leaving Celestia alone in the world.

Celestia then began to wonder what it would be like to introduce Star to Abaven. Would Star be frightened by Celestia's beast? Would they get along, or would Abaven be skeptical of Star?

Upon reaching their destination, Celestia hopped from Star's back, removing the satchel from Star's side and placing it on the blanketed ground. Star lay down on the grass, Celestia propping her head against the horse and glanced at her "brother".

She found herself burning with a jealous rage, at first. She should have been raised in a castle with two loving parents and all of the comforts of a privileged life... but instead she had grown up self-isolated in a tower. As her heart filled with bitterness towards Maverick, who lived the life that she had always dreamed of, she suddenly realized that he had forsaken it all to come in search of her. In fact, he was definitely too young and inexperienced to have left the castle in the dead of night in search of a sister he had just barely learned of.

Ever since they had met, he had been helpful, kind, and considerate (even if he was a bit clumsy and paranoid). He truly cared for her, even if he did not really know her. It was not his choice for her to have a life apart from him. If anything, she could tell that he wished she had been a part of that life and would change the past if he had the chance. Knowing that, Celestia allowed her resentment towards Maverick to slip away and drifted asleep for the third time that night.

Only seconds after snores erupted from the horse's lips and Celestia's breaths slowed, Maverick jolted awake, his fingers digging into the dirt beneath him as he stared ahead. Confusion tugged at his consciousness as his dream replayed through his mind relentlessly.

Maverick watched as his father embraced a little girl, looking deeply into her eyes before leading her to a horse-drawn carriage. His father picked her up, smiling at her one last time before handing her to one of the waiting servants.

"Where am I going, *daddy*? Are you coming?" Maverick's father shook his head.

"You're not safe here, darling. These men will take you somewhere safe. I can't come with you, I have to protect the people in my kingdom. But I will come to get you one day, okay?"

The little girl nodded, obviously confused as servants seated and secured her in a carriage. Maverick could hear the clacking of horse hooves on the cobblestone road and watched as the carriage disappeared.

Maverick seemed to hear the muffled voices of his parents in the distance, shushing him and rocking him for a reason he didn't know. Then, everything was silent.

Maverick's heart pounded and he immediately turned to gaze at Celestia, who was sleeping propped against Star. It wasn't a dream, it was a memory.

He felt a searing pain in his chest and cried out, tears filling his eyes as he suddenly recognized her for the first time.

So much had occurred in the past few weeks that left him grappling with understanding everything. Ever since he had stumbled across Celestia and her dragon, she had treated him like he was a pest. She had ordered him to leave her alone, and yet suddenly she was claiming that she was his missing sister. How could this be possible? And yet, he had left the castle in search of a long lost sister, so it must be true. He shook his head, trying to clear his mind from the muddle of thoughts, hoping to separate his memories from his nightmares and wondering if they were one and the same.

Here she was, lying in front of him in plain sight, yet it took him days just to recognize her as his own sister. Maverick paused, wondering if he should have tried to find out more before he left the castle. Why had she been sent away and locked in a tower? Was it because he was born and his father had wanted a son to rule over their kingdom? Was it because someone wanted to harm Celestia?

But then Maverick remembered, he remembered his father mentioning a King and his son, Prince Lucier. A few months prior, Maverick's father had asked him to embark on the quest that Lucier had created. He told him he should pursue the lost princess, but Maverick had told him he had no interest in doing so. Lucier had sent several groups of people in search of the princess, all so he could bring her back and betroth her. Maverick suddenly understood why. Because Celestia was older than Maverick, the throne was hers as soon as his parents passed on. But, if Lucier could marry Celestia, the throne would be his for the taking. He would automatically have rule over all of the kingdom's subjects and obtain the monocratic domination he desired.

Then Maverick wondered if keeping their kingdom safe was worth all of the suffering that Celestia had to endure. All of the emotions she'd kept to herself seemed to stream into the poor prince's heart. He felt her pain. He felt her loneliness. He felt her despair.

And he hated himself for not remembering her. But most of all, he hated his parents for not telling him of her existence. For not giving him the chance to grow up with his big sister.

Maverick felt himself pulled into an embrace. He didn't bother to look up, just curled into a ball. Maverick didn't even have to say a word; Celestia seemed to understand his reasons for crying.

"*I'm here now.*" She whispered, holding her younger brother closer to her. Even Star forgave him for just that moment and lifted her head to gaze at him sympathetically. She neighed, as though reassuring him he would be okay. The siblings sat wrapped in each other's arms for the first time since they could remember.

Maverick felt complete, as though a missing puzzle piece in his heart had just been found. And even though he hadn't had her his whole life, he was glad to have her by his side at that moment.

Eventually, Star nudged herself between their bodies, seeming to want in on the hug. She could almost feel the waves of emotion, of relief and contentment, wafting off the siblings, which drew her towards them. Celestia couldn't help laughing, and even Maverick allowed a small smile to pull at his lips.

He had no more reason to cry. She was here and she wasn't leaving anytime soon. With this thought, he allowed the smallest of laughs to escape his lips.

"Let's go home." Celestia spoke, images of the long forgotten castle forming in her mind. Maverick nodded his head, smiling. They finally had a destination.

The siblings hauled themselves onto Star's back as she began to trot toward the trail. Digging through their bag, Celestia pulled out a fist full of berries and divided them into thirds, passing some of them to Maverick, feeding a couple to Star, and then popping the rest into her mouth. Maverick ate them gladly, gulping them down in seconds and, afterwards, gripping onto Celestia's shoulders, hoping he wouldn't fall. Having her so close seemed surreal now, as though maybe he was just dreaming. Maybe his sister wasn't right in front of him.

But Maverick had never felt such greater joy than when he realized he wasn't dreaming. He wasn't going to wake up and have her torn from his grasp once more. She was there, and she would stay there.

He decided then that he would wait and allow his parents to tell her the truth themselves- it wasn't his place to explain to Celestia that their parents were willing to sacrifice her for the betterment of their kingdom.

Pulled from his silent reverie, he bounced up and down on the saddle as Star glided between the trees, along the twisted trail.

Star's hooves kicked up a cloud of dust, making it difficult to breath and causing them to break into a fit of coughing. Even Star had to stop every once in a while to sneeze.

A gentle breeze began to form, brushing the cloud of dust behind them, clearing the air, and allowing them to inhale the sweet scent of damp leaves. The atmosphere remained quiet, only the faint sound of falling water in the background as they continued their search.

Eventually, as the sun began its rise above the mountain top, they came to an opening between the trees. A large, barren and lifeless meadow spread before them. Celestia smiled, holding her fingers to her mouth and allowing a loud whistle to play past her lips. Maverick dismounted, helping Celestia down as large gusts of air whipped towards them. Star reared backward, neighing in fright as her front legs pawed the air. Celesia rushed to calm the startled animal, who was quick to quiet as long as Celestia remained by her side. Although Star had only just accepted Celestia as a new companion, there was something about her, something warm and powerful, that made Star want to listen.

Once Star's breaths had returned to normal, Celestia gently moved from the horse's side, leaving Maverick beside her instead. After days of waiting, they finally got to see her beast once more.

The first thing Abaven noticed as he landed were the cuts and scrapes marking Celestia's arms. He immediately vowed to destroy whoever had harmed her. He could feel the tight breaths she drew and the sharp, scratchy feeling in her throat every time she swallowed. Abaven had trusted that she would be fine on her own, but clearly that was not the case.

But then he saw the giddy smile on her face and realized that the princess was absolutely radiant, despite her disheveled appearance. He dismissed his raging thoughts and became grateful, instead, that she was joyful. Her beast gently lowered his head, lying down in exhaustion from the constant flight.

"You missed so much." Celestia whispered, petting his snout.

"I found my brother."

Chapter 14

"We are heading in the wrong direction,
Maverick." Celestia stated flatly from her perch on
the horse behind her brother. Maverick grasped the
reins and urged Star forward.

"No, we're going the right way. I know it." He
adjusted his grip on Star's reins, guiding her along
the trail. Celestia was certain they had been going in
circles for what seemed like hours.

"We were at that tree five minutes ago! I think
I should lead Star." Although Celestia instinctively
felt she could trust Star and Maverick with anything,
she wasn't sure Maverick had a very good sense of
direction. Star seemed to bob her head in agreement,
but Maverick only pouted.

"Stop doubting me." And with that, he
tugged on Star's reins, veering off the trail and
leading her down a different path. The forest became
denser with each step they took; crows screeched and
shadows lengthened. They seemed to shout 'Go
away' and their caws became deafening. Celestia felt

a twisted, sick feeling inside her gut, as though protesting each step further into the forest.

"Maverick, I don't think..." Maverick shushed her, loosening his grip on Star's reins.

"Did you hear that?" he whispered. Celestia strained her ears, trying to calm the terrible feeling in her stomach and allowing her brother to take charge, for most likely the last time. She couldn't hear anything, other than the call of the crows, and she wondered if Maverick was just messing with her.

But then the leaves began to shake, the branches above them twisting and turning, knotting together and nearly creating a barrier, shading the ground in a thick mat of shadows. Small rays of sunlight peeked through the shadowy barrier, providing just barely enough light for the travelers to see by.

Even the tree trunks began to look darker and drearier; spookier, even. Eyes seemed to peek out from the spaces between branches and shrubbery.

Although Celestia felt the urge to turn around, wondering if they were being followed, she allowed Maverick to continue down that path. Maybe, just maybe, he'd realize by himself that he wasn't exactly skilled when it comes to navigation.

Celestia began to hum, hoping to keep the gnawing fear at bay. Maverick listened to her soft humming, the tune tugging at a faint memory. He gradually joined in, catching onto the tune almost immediately. A strange sense of Deja vu twisted through his thoughts. He knew the song, but he had no idea how he knew it.

Celestia was immediately surprised when Maverick began to hum along with her. She was amazed he would remember something from so long ago.

"Mommy?" The little princess cried out, sitting up in her bed and staring at the wall across from her. Her eyes were wide and frightened, and she didn't dare move.

"What's the matter, darling?" Her mother's voice sounded from the doorway, causing the little girl to turn her head in relief. Her mother's features were worn and tired, but a gentle smile still graced the queen's face.

"Did you have a bad dream?" The queen asked, noticing the girl's frightened features. She nodded her head, watching as her mother neared the bed, holding a sleeping infant in her arms. As the queen sat on the mattress, Celestia scooted next to her mother and gazed at her sleeping baby brother.

"If I sing you a song, will you go to sleep?" the queen asked. Celestia nodded, hurriedly ducking under the covers and waiting for her mother to sing the demons away.

The little baby boy in her mother's arms awoke, his bright green eyes locking with Celestia's. Her mother, smiling at both children, tucked the little boy next to his sister and watched as Celestia pulled her little brother closer. With a tired smile, the queen began to sing.

"*Twinkle twinkle little star...*" Celestia pouted, cutting her mother off with a groan. The queen laughed and then began singing again, Celestia's eyes twinkling as she listened to the lyrics.

"*I will make you queen of everything you see,*
I'll give you what is yours,
I'll help you to be free.
Although these soldiers might break through,
The barriers I've built for you,
Someday soon,

You will be with me.
All these monsters without a clue,
But I'll just fight them off for you,
Just stick with me,
And you'll stay free.
I will make you queen of everything you see..."

Celestia hummed along to the melody and even the infant beside her made small gurgling sounds, as though he was trying to sing with them to. The queen's angelic voice faded in and out of their minds, until Celestia finally fell asleep. Her little brother closed his eyes, as though mimicking her actions, and fell unconscious only seconds afterward. The queen stopped singing, gazing at her children and allowing a small smile to grace her lips.

She stood from the bed, leaving the two siblings bundled in blankets. She kissed them both on the forehead and then quietly left the bedchamber and closed the door behind her, allowing the room to be encased, once more, in the darkness of night.

Celestia smiled at the memory, closing her eyes and humming again. She pressed her forehead against Maverick's back, her arms hanging loosely around his torso. He continued humming along with her until Star suddenly stopped in her tracks. She gave a loud frightened neigh, jolting the siblings from their reverie and causing Celestia to sit upright, eyes afraid and unsteady. Star sensed something in the darkness that they couldn't.

All the crows seemed to screech in warning, flying away from the area as Star took off at a full gallop, ignoring Maverick's attempts to control her. The trees grew more dense as they galloped onward, Star swerving in and out of the grasping branches. Heavy breaths escaped the horse's mouth as she forced herself forward, Celestia and Maverick holding onto her for dear life.

Branches and twigs snapped behind them, proving they were indeed being followed. Celestia risked a glance behind her as she clung to Maverick's shoulders. Yards behind her, tearing through the trees, was a creature encased in wispy shadows. The texture of it's skin was like that of a cloud, drifting with the wind and constantly shifting position and placement. It had four, brawny legs, much like

Abavens, and bounded closer to them with every step. It's long, barbed claws shredded the ground beneath it, sending chunks of dirt and grass flying in every direction. The creature was nearly twice the size of Star, and it's head took the appearance of a wolf's, with a long snout and jagged teeth. Although the creature had no eyes, it seemed to be looking directly at Celestia and it's lips pulled into a menacing grin that sent shivers down her spine.

Celestia wanted to turn away, but her arms and legs had seemed to stiffen; she couldn't move. Her heart beat loudly in her ears as the creature crept closer, goosebumps crawling up her skin. A light dizziness overcame her, causing her to clench her eyes shut. She attempted to erase the image of the creature's toothy grin from her mind, but the picture of the eyeless beast was so vivid in her imagination, it was as if her eyes were still open.

"Go faster, Star," Celestia yelped, her voice trembling. She finally recovered from the tightness in her muscles, quickly turning her body and wrapping her arms tightly around Maverick's torso, too afraid to open her eyes. Maverick could feel Celestia shuddering behind him, and worriedly egged Star on as well.

"What was back there?" He inquired, but Celestia found herself unable to answer him. She couldn't will herself to swallow, couldn't slow her breath, and couldn't utter another syllable.

Maverick gazed quickly behind them just as the creature disappeared from view.

"Celestia," he spoke, softly, "there's nothing there."

Celestia blinked, sitting confusedly upright. Willing her wild heart rate to calm, she hastily glimpsed behind them. She felt her grip on Maverick loosen as she was greeted with the surprising image of nothing. Where had it gone?

Just to be safe, Celestia urged Star to continue galloping for at least another mile until allowing her to slow to a light tread.

Celestia jumped carefully off the horse and scanned the area, haunting images of the creature overpowering her thoughts. Maverick followed her movements, jumping off Star and moving alongside his sister. Finding it secure, Celestia grabbed the reins and walked ahead of Star, who was still jittery, snorting and shaking her head as if to chase the demons away. Celestia considered telling Maverick what she had seen, but then thought otherwise. She didn't want his fears to feed off of her own.

"I guess I didn't really know where I was going," Maverick mumbled. Celestia laughed at his remark, hoping to ease the nightmares that still flashed through her mind.

"Maybe next time, I should lead." Celestia suggested. Maverick said nothing, but silently agreed.

As much as he wanted to believe he was, Maverick was no good with navigation. He would never admit that, but he was quite sure Celestia already knew.

Chapter 15

Star trotted giddily, having regained her strength since the beast had stopped chasing them. Star seemed eager to continue onward and Celestia could easily relate.

Peering ahead, the dirt pathway began to widen, the trees seemed to bow toward one another in a respectful demeanor.

As she continued walking, Celestia saw that there were murals, dozens of stories, carved into the bark of each tree. Each branch was different in its own, unique way. The carvings seemed to grow throughout the whole tree, over its branches, trunk, and even its leaves. Walking on, she studied each carving, the images flashing through her mind, piecing together like a whole storybook. From what Celestia could piece together form the murals, it appeared to be a history of the villagers and their kingdom.

"Celestia," Maverick started, his voice hushed. She glanced in his direction and, although he uttered no word, she realized that he recognized the place. It meant something. Maverick was staring at the trees with nostalgia, memories clouding him still from when he was a child. In fact, Maverick was quite sure that he had visited this kingdom only months before with his father. They had been on a trip to negotiate some trading routes and Maverick had grown rather fond of the kingdom while they were in it.

Maverick suddenly began to swell with hope. Maybe they could receive a welcome, directions, equipment of some sort. Maybe they could have a saddle made for Abaven! Maybe, just maybe, they would no longer have to travel the journey on foot.

As branches began binding together, the trees reached towards each other and formed an arch. The carvings seemed to grow with intensity, depicting wars and mythical beasts that appeared to be arriving at the borders of the mystical kingdom. But Celestia immediately disregarded the strange murals as they came upon a small clearing. She cast her eyes forward, and hope died immediately. Celestia couldn't help the gasp that escaped her mouth, and Maverick's own lip trembled.

The whole area was a charred mass of collapsed stone and burnt timbers. What used to be a towering, lavish castle was now just piles of crumbling stone walls and shattered shards of glass, lining the ground around them. There were obvious signs of struggle, and it seemed as though beneath the piles of rubbish were the bodies of those who had once inhabited the area. Their possessions were mangled and forgotten, mounds of burnt books and broken furniture scattered everywhere. Cottages, stretching for miles among the trees, were burnt and collapsing into piles of ash. The whole kingdom had fallen.

A few rooms still stood, bravely towering above the rest of the crumbled castle. Celestia and Maverick walked toward the remains, stepping over debris and decay, avoiding the vines and plants that creeped out of the ground. Star stayed behind, neighing in remorse at the lost empire.

Celestia heard a crack beneath her foot and slowly looked down, afraid of what she might see. A punctured skull was lying beside her shoe, and she frantically stepped back and looked away. What could have possibly happened here? As Celestia continued exploring the ruins, she discovered dozens of other skulls fractured by the crumbling bricks and buried beneath layers of dust and grime. In all of the years she spent locked in her tower, she had never once seen anything as gruesome as this. It was then that Celestia wondered if this is what her father had meant to protect her from. Celestia looked beside her, observing Maverick. She could tell he was focusing all of his energy at that moment on not screaming or crying.

"I used to visit this kingdom as a child. It was such a kingdom full of innocent people with hopes, dreams, and hearts full of love. I just don't understand how it has come to such an utter destruction."

Celestia nodded her head in agreement, no kingdom deserved a downfall such as this.

Avoiding stepping on any more skulls or bone fragments, Celestia had finally made it through the sea of debris. She gazed at what looked like the remainder of a throne room. Three walls still stood, one holding a large window, streaks of colored light streaming through what remained of the cracked stained glass.

A throne sat directly beneath the window, untouched and shining with pride. Even the velvety red cushion lining its seat was barely scathed, only a small tear on the very tip. Celestia walked toward the throne, watching her footing. Maverick, who was walking behind her, kicked through a pile of rubble on the floor. He stopped, noticing something glinting in the charred debris and bent for a closer look, reaching out and brushing away a coat of dust and dirt. It was a gold coin. As Maverick reached out to pick up the coin he saw a charred leather pouch with more gold spilling out. Without pausing to think, Maverick quickly pocketed the bag of coins, knowing they could come in handy in the future.

Celestia looked down at the shining golden throne. Although it disgusted her, she felt intrigued by it. Her hand, hesitantly, began to stroke the gold handles, dragging delicately along its interior. Images flashed through her mind, nearly too fast for her to acknowledge. But she managed to remember some of the fleeting images of a burning castle, collapsing cottages, and frantic, frightened villagers. Immediately, she separated herself from the piece of furniture, the images abruptly stopping.

Celestia raced out of the throne room towards where Star was waiting, far from the debris. Maverick bolted after her, concerned for her well being.

"Are you alright?" He inquired, and Celestia mounted the horse as if to say: let's get out of here.

Maverick hopped on in agreement, and without another word, they continued forward.

As they wove in between crumbled roads and broken homes, flashes of the vision creeped back into Celestia's mind. Only now, the images and pictures were more heavy and coherent. Hundreds of terror-stricken villagers hustled and hid throughout the trees and disintegrating abodes. There was an extensive heat, causing even Celestia to break out a sweat. Flames erupted from castle windows and stones dislodged, falling like rain from the gloomy sky. The thick, blinding smoke seemed to have a mind of its own, and although many people clawed and blew at it, the smoke engulfed them anyway. Soldiers marched in, maiming and stabbing anyone who stood in their way. A man, in the middle of their battalion, was perched on a black steed with a crown adorning his head. He smirked, his hateful eyes seeming to bore into Celestia's.

The entire spectacle was too much for Celestia to fathom, so she shook the thoughts from her head and forced the memories away, refocusing her attention to the road ahead of her. After a while, to their relief, they finally left the blackened remains behind and went through a pathway between the trees, their trunks arching and fading into the distance. Maverick studied the carvings but didn't seem to notice Celestia's uneasy stance.

Celestia shivered and glanced at the sky, half expecting it to be stormy. Instead, a small, white particle landed on her nose. As she tried to focus on it to examine it, it disappeared. The thing was accompanied by two more. They soon dissolved, disappearing from sight. Furrowing her eyebrows, Celestia studied the sky again, noticing several of these white things were now falling from the clouds.

"What is that stuff?" Celestia asked, Maverick followed her gaze and gave a hearty laugh. Then, out of respect for the princess, he quieted himself. She'd been locked away all her life, of course she wouldn't know what snow was. It never snowed by their kingdom, let alone the tower in which she was once held captive in. Celestia examined the trees, their leaves were gone and their branches were bare. Some were covered in this white substance, yet Celestia couldn't understand why.

"They're called snowflakes. The white coating the ground is snow. This is what happens to rain when the weather gets really cold." Celestia nodded, slowly, as though trying to comprehend the fact there were more elements to the earth than she knew of.

"It's basically frozen water, or soft ice." Maverick added, as though that fact could clear up any misunderstandings Celestia may have had.

As Star trotted forward, the line of trees began to recede, barren snow for as far as the eye could see. In no time at all, there wasn't another tree in sight; only looming frost-covered mountains were visible. Celestia watched as her breath clouded outward, creating fog. The cold pricked her skin, but she didn't seem to notice the temperature change. Even Maverick seemed joyful at the fact they were surrounded by a field of snow and leapt off Star and onto the ground.

Star seemed suddenly discouraged, giving a low neigh of disapproval, knowing she'd have to carry her two friends through the snow and over rocks. Both of which hurt her hooves.

Celestia dismounted Star, patting her back reassuringly and walking beside Maverick. The cold immediately engulfed her feet, causing her teeth to chatter. But she enjoyed the unrecognizable sensation. Celestia kicked up snow, laughing and putting the pictures of fire and war out of her mind. Maverick shrugged, doing the same as her. Even Star seemed a little giddy, and leapt into pace with her two human friends.

Celestia picked up handfuls of the cold icy substance and threw it in the air, watching with excitement as it fluttered down and covered the three of them. Celestia's eyes twinkled, her blonde hair filled with dozens of snowflakes, sparkling and glittering like diamonds.

Maverick smiled at his sister, his hair disheveled and small flakes of snow melting on his skin. His cheeks were rosy and his clothes were stained with dirt, sweat, and water. But he didn't seem to care. And the best part was, neither did Celestia or Star.

Chapter 16

Star neighed quietly beside her companions, as though urging them forward. At the sound of the horse's gentle reminder, the siblings began walking once more. They tramped through the snow, their feet gradually sinking deeper with every step. Their smiles gradually faded, their excitement dissipating as they realized the icy froth around them was becoming increasingly difficult to travel through. The air became more crisp the further they trekked, and mounds of snow quickly began to pile up around them. The dusky clouds blotted out any signs of the sun or moon and they no longer knew whether it was morning or afternoon.

"We should find some shelter, soon," Celestia advised, and Maverick nodded in agreement.

Celestia's body wasn't accustomed to such frosty weather, and her arms had turned an unhealthy shade of white. The cold became so intense that it felt as though she was walking on fiery pins and needles.

It almost seemed as though they had been slogging through the snow for weeks, months even. But as they continued trudging forwards, Star in the lead, they realized they had only been traveling for a handful of hours. Celestia and Maverick linked arms, as though their combined body heat could immediately warm them; that barely helped.

Snowflakes fell rapidly from the sky, the snow collecting until the three travelers were knee deep in the icy cold drifts. Celestia was practically blue, her whole body numb from her ears to her feet. A shiver racked through her body every few seconds, causing her to stumble or freeze until she could persuade herself to continue onward. Celestia, not in the slightest bit prepared for such weather, felt as though life was slipping through her, melting into the snow with every step she forced. Even Maverick, who had the advantage of thicker clothes, seemed deathly pale and exhausted. Celestia copied Mavericks movements, rubbing her hands together every few seconds for heat. Sadly, that did nothing but send shards of pain through her frozen hands.

Finally, the cold was unbearable, and Celestia collapsed in the snow, her legs refusing to move another step in the full force blizzard. Even though the snow was beautiful, it definitely had its downside.

Maverick sat beside her in the snow; even his body was beginning to fail him. Star stopped and gazed at her friends, neighing in encouragement, but couldn't motivate the two to move or speak.

Exhausted and freezing, the snow seemed attracted to them and covered them inch after inch in white layers. Celestia's thoughts had become foggy and her body was overwhelmed with the desire to sleep, but she knew she had to do something.

In her frozen stupor, Celestia slowly came to the conclusion that Abaven had the ability to protect and keep them warm. She forced herself to sit up, snow falling from her hair and into her lap. She attempted to lift her fingers to her mouth, so she could whistle for her dragon, but her hands and lips were frozen; she couldn't make a sound. Shaking herself off, Celestia ignored the prickling pain and rubbed her hands together in an attempt to thaw them. She repeated this motion for several minutes, fighting ceaselessly against sleep. Eventually, Celestia puckered her numb lips and let out a hushed whistle for Abaven.

By some miracle, Abaven managed to hear the muted whistle. He swooped towards the direction of the high pitched noise. His eyes were nearly blinded by all the white, but he managed to spot a black dot below him. He dove towards it and his wings folded into his back as he glided downwards.

The white sheet below became fresh snow, the black dot becoming a princess with shining golden hair. Star was curled beside the siblings and they huddled together for warmth. Abaven allowed his wings to slow his fall, stretching them out and landing gracefully in the snow beside them.

The three looked up at the sudden noise, forcing themselves from their places in the frost. Celestia was the first to wobble forward, stumbling toward her dragon with open arms. As she stood in front of him, he lay down, allowing her to climb onto his scaly back. She used what little strength she had left to lift herself halfway up his wing and he nudged her up the rest of the way.

Next came Maverick, stumbling through the snow. His hand was looped through Stars reins, pulling her with him. Star reared back, frightened again by the beast, and fought against Maverick's grip on her reigns. Celestia called to the horse, soothing and reassuring the horse of her safety.

"Star, remember Abaven? You've met before! I know that appearances can be daunting, but Abaven is a very loving and trustworthy creature. I hope that you will become great friends." Star glanced warily at Abaven, but he flashed her a large toothy grin in return. Star quickly realized she was being ridiculous and could feel warmth and trust radiating in the air between them.

Abaven slowly extended his wing towards Star and she trudged forward, nudging his wing as a declaration of friendship.

Maverick briskly climbed to the top of the towering beast. He ran across its back and over to his sister, sitting beside her.

Star, realizing she could easily slip from the beast's back, trotted ahead of him as he lifted himself up. Abaven began walking forward, clearing a trail in the snow with each step and heading in the direction of the mountain ahead. Star followed behind in Abaven's tracks, grateful that he had cleared the way through the deep snow so that she didn't have to work so hard.

They speedily reached the mountain, the tip disappearing into the smoky sky above and towering over them. Abaven allowed a puff of smoke to escape his mouth, warning Star to move out of his way, and she cautiously did. He lay himself down, allowing Cestia and Maverick to easily slide down his tail. They stumbled into the cold slush, rolling headfirst and landing in it with a plop. Celestia seemed to laugh, but it only came out as a puff of fog.

Maverick and Celestia stood, brushing the snow from their clothes. Celestia ran towards Star, Maverick following after her. They left no footprints, sliding and tumbling across the ice. Now, skidding beside Star, they followed Abaven toward a large crevice in the looming rock.

Abaven blew a quick huff of fire, lighting the torches lining the walls of the unoccupied cave and allowing his companions to enter before poking his head inside. A large rock jutted over the entrance to the cave, serving as protection to the dragon from the falling snow and biting wind. With Abaven covering the entrance to the cave, the group was both safe and warm.

Celestia lay against Abaven's neck, humming to herself as Maverick searched through their sack for any edible foods. He found the berries, but they were frozen solid. The bread and other items he had originally packed for the journey were frozen, mushy, and falling apart, so he warmed the berries and distributed them evenly to everyone. That'd have to do, for now.

As Star settled down and Maverick lay against the horse's side, the two humans began to converse, sharing short stories. Celestia talked of her new love for snow (even though it was freezing cold, it was still amazing), and Maverick told stories of when he was just a little child, playing in the snow and learning to ride a horse. Of course, he had many more childhood memories than Celestia had of her own. But she listened intently, feeling as though she was a part of his past and she had never been separated from her brother in the first place.

They fell asleep hours later, the darkness having fallen outside. Celestia could see the stars gleaming through a small space between her beast and the tip of the cave. And so she fell asleep, her heart filled with a tremendous joy she had never before known existed.

Chapter 17

Celestia, waking up with a yawn and a stretch, wasted no time and got straight to work. She snatched the burnt out torches from the wall, placing them in the satchel lying beside her brother. Maverick had informed her the evening before that there were only short periods of good weather in the mountains, so Celestia knew they had to begin traveling as quickly as they could. She hurriedly woke Maverick, but it took a lot of effort to wake up Star. For a moment, they even feared she wasn't going to awake... but still succeeded after a number of tries.

After finally readying themselves for the weather, Maverick and Celestia mounted Star and the horse walked unsteadily toward Abaven. The dragon's eyes snapped open and he smiled at his friends as he slipped from the cave's entrance. He flapped his enormous wings, shaking off the snow layering his body.

Although Abaven was able to survive the night, protecting them from the frosty weather, he was not warm-blooded like his companions. If he did not fly somewhere warm soon, he could easily fall ill and die. Celestia beckoned him to leave, to get some sun and energize. Although he offered, Celestia and Maverick refused to ride along with him knowing that Star would be left behind.

With one last glimpse at them, Abaven departed and launched himself into the air, flying behind a layer of fluffy clouds. He had the strong instinct to return, to travel alongside for a few hours longer and make sure they were alright... but he knew that Celestia wouldn't allow him to. She wanted him to be safe and although it was hard for her to travel through the snow, she knew that it was a more perilous journey for her dragon. Abaven watched protectively as their figures became nothing but little specks of color as he rose in elevation.

After watching the beast's departure, Star began walking. She was soon at the cave's entrance, the freezing snow cascading over her hooves. Stumbling into the frothy snowfall, she carefully stomped through the icy drifts. The journey was becoming increasingly strenuous slogging through snow, and Star missed having Abaven to clear the path for her. At some points, the snow was even piled all the way up to Star's chest, but she heaved forward anyway. She felt it was her duty to get the siblings to a safe place, even if she didn't quite know where that place was.

The trio of travelers slogged on through the blinding snow and biting wind, losing all track of time. They would travel as far as they could during the daylight hours, then seek shelter when the sun began to set. Each morning they began the battle through the ever-growing drifts of snow, and each evening they prayed to find a rocky outcrop or copse of trees where they could shelter for the night. Had it only been three days? Four? Celestia only knew that Star was weakened and exhausted, and they needed to find food soon. Often the siblings, who could sense the toll the weather was taking on Star, jumped from her back and instead hiked beside her. They guided her forward, noticing how with every passing day her trudging seemed more uncertain and more unbalanced.

The bitter weather finally seemed to catch up with them. The clouds fused together, darkening in color the further they traveled into the mountain range. Snowflakes whizzed past their heads as gusts of wind slashed against them. Celestia noticed Star waning, and urged her onward. Star's utter exhaustion was taking over, and she couldn't handle the snow and the inconstant weather all together. She had been treading through slush for days on end without much of a break in between, and it had exhausted her beyond comprehension.

Celestia thought perhaps if they rested for a little while Star would be able to continue on, but the moment they stopped moving the animal collapsed into a heap in the blinding snow. Celestia and Maverick tried desperately to urge Star to rise as both the wind and the snow turned into a full-force blizzard. It was so loud, in fact, that whistling for Abaven was hopeless... and they would have to rescue themselves.

Celestia pulled Star's reins while Maverick pushed on Star's side, desperately trying to raise the horse to her feet. She neighed in protest, her whines so weak that they were scarcely audible. Grudgingly, the siblings laid Star down in the snow, knowing that their effort to assist her was to no avail.

Celestia lowered to the horse's level, gazing at Star feebly as she panted gravelly, her breath wisping out as labored puffs in the chilly air. Maverick, who had gone ahead in an attempt to find shelter, was now sensing the others were far behind him, so he stopped in his tracks and turned around.

Noticing Celestia's lack of movement, Maverick leapt through the snow and to his sister's side in a matter of seconds. Maverick tugged her arm.

"We have to keep moving, Celestia, or we will freeze!" He urged her, knowing full well that the weather would only get worse.

Celestia ignored Maverick's pleading and instead rocked Star's body back and forth in an attempt to get the horse to move.

"We can't just leave her here! She'll die if we leave her." Celestia stated, helplessly gazing down at the horse. Star had come so far, she'd pushed herself so hard to help the siblings on their journey. Star was a strong and determined horse, and Celestia suspected she at least had *some* will to get back up again.

But Star just lay there, panting, the slow rise and fall of her chest jittery. Celestia, despite the cold eating at her skin and the snow that latched to her hair, lay down in the snow next to Star, petting the horse's mane softly.

Maverick leaned down, closely observing Star and watching sorrowfully as her eyes began to glaze over. She wasn't going to make it. He sat next to his companions, watching as Star neighed frighteningly. She knew if she fell asleep, she wouldn't wake up.

Celestia spoke to the scared little horse reassuringly, pretending she was calm and her heart wasn't aching. It took every ounce of her being to push away the tears building in her eyes and smile for her friend.

"You'll be fine," She lied, her voice hushed and nurturing. 'You just go ahead and rest here for a few minutes. You'll be ready to move in no time!" Star took comfort in her false words, gratefulness entering the horse's eyes as with one last breath, she closed her eyes and her chest ceased to move. And then she was motionless.

Maverick shuffled to his sister's side and held her close. He had no words to express the regret and guilt he felt in knowing that Star could no longer make it to the end of the journey, and he had not been able to save her.

But Maverick had come to his senses, and knew that while Star might not be able to make it, they still could. And if they were to survive, they would have to leave.

"We have to go," Maverick stood, pulling at Celestia's arm in hopes she, too, would see the reason and logic behind such a request.

But Celestia wouldn't move, lost in her mind. She couldn't breath; couldn't blink. She stared into the soulless eyes of her friend, wondering suddenly if this was the evil that her father had locked her away to protect her from. She wrapped her arms around the horse's neck, begging her not to leave. Begging the horse to rise again.

But no amount of love, of hope, or of friendship could save Star from the bringer of death.

Maverick, unaware of the brick that had taken place of Celestia's heart, pulled Celestia to her feet and helped her walk in her weakened state.

"We can't just leave her." Celestia urged, but however much she wanted to believe her Star was still alive, she knew that it wasn't true. Her Star had fallen, and its light had faded.

"We at least need to bury her..." She choked, tears finally finding their way to her eyes, blotting out the world around her. The ground was much too hard to dig through, and so she knew that burying her Star couldn't be done. Glancing back at the spot where Star had died, she saw that nature had taken over for her and had covered Star's body in a thick layer of snow, effectively providing a winter's grave for the brave horse.

Celestia felt the unfamiliar weight of death placed upon her shoulders, but she didn't know if she had the strength to carry it.

Chapter 18

The weather only worsened, to the point that Celestia couldn't even see Maverick beside her. His hand in her own was the only indication that he wasn't lost. She tightened her grip subconsciously... she couldn't lose Maverick, too.

The intense weather only added to the difficulty of the journey. Celestia's bare shoes were soaked through and her feet were numb with cold, causing her to stumble with nearly every step. The wind pushed against her and it took all of her will-power just to stay on course.

Celestia could feel the cold practically seeping into her bones. If this continued much longer, she'd be a goner.

Suddenly, as if she had called in an unspoken favor, the wind and snow seemed to stop altogether. Celestia could, surprisingly, see Maverick beside her. Gazing around them, Celestia realized they had entered a narrow canyon between two sharply rising rocks. It was almost like a cave, guarding them from the elements, but with an added bonus of actually being able to see the sky above them. The siblings carefully made their way through the narrow opening, the storm raging behind them and giving them a much needed break from the snow and cold.

As they stepped out of the narrow mountain pass, in the distance they spotted a frost layered village. Dozens of small abodes were clustered together, barely visible in the endless field of white. Despite their exhaustion, the siblings felt a renewed energy and began pushing through the snow in haste, racing each other to the town, fueled by pure adrenaline.

When they finally approached the town's western entrance, they took a moment to examine their surroundings. The large wood and stone dwellings seemed to be enveloped in a layer of frost. The buildings were quite similar in stature, with the exception of a few towering over the others.

The snow seemed to melt away as they reached a stone pathway. Although it was covered in frost, it was thankfully clear of the knee-deep snow they had trudged through to reach their haven. They continued walking and were soon at the town's center.

Two people passed them on the street, but they averted their eyes and pointedly ignored Celestia and Maverick. The people hastily disappeared into a house, slamming the door behind them with a loud bang and the snap of a lock. Small children peered at the siblings from the windows before being snatched away by their parents.

The villagers seemed to be threatened by the two travelers; who were shivering with cold there in the center of their town. Celestia walked up the steps to the front porch of one of the homes and knocked on the door. No answer. She knocked again. Still no answer. Maverick tried the neighboring house, but the knocks echoed unwelcomingly back at him. Maverick gazed around, realizing that it wasn't doing them any good to knock on the doors of houses. Instead, they should be looking for a shop, or an inn, where they would be used to travelers stopping by.

Maverick spotted a frosted sign dangling from one of the taller buildings and instantly, out of curiosity, began walking toward it. Celestia, too, noticed the sign and began to walk with him. The word 'Tailor' was painted in faded letters on its surface.

Celestia reached the door of the building and knocked. Maverick, realizing that Celestia had been locked away in a tower for years and didn't know what a shop was, reached out, grasped the door latch, pushed the door open and guided Celestia inside. The first thing Celestia noted was the warmth. The warmth and the light. She stopped just inside the door, marveling at the heat that enfolded her.

Her whole body savored the heat, especially after a week's worth of snow, snow... and more snow. Maverick pushed her gently aside, making room for himself. As the siblings walked forward, their hands and feet began to tingle and they felt as though their hands and feet were being pricked by sharp pins and needles. Maverick directed Celestia over to the pot belly stove, sitting in the corner of the shop, and they both held their hands out to warm them. The snow slowly melted from their hair and faces, steam gently rising from their sodden clothing as the heat from the stove welcomed them.

The cashier took immediate notice of their appearance, they looked as though they had been traveling for days. The cashier wondered where they had come from and where they were heading. What had brought them to his town?

"What can I help you with?" called the cashier.

"Do you have a winter selection?" Maverick inquired. The cashier smiled and nodded, pointing toward an aisle of thick cloaks and shirts in response. Maverick nodded thankfully and then guided Celestia over to the clothes, trying to find something her size.

Maverick grabbed two pairs of stitched pants and two long sleeved shirts and coats and piled them in Celestia's arms, pushing her toward the counter. He fetched a new satchel, two pairs of fur lined boots and added a stack of warm clothing for himself.

"That'll be two crowns," stated the cashier. Maverick reached into the worn bag hanging at his waist, pulling out a handful of tarnished gold pieces and placed one of them on the counter. He carefully set the rest of the coins back in the pouch, taking notice of the Celestia's gaze, fixated on the gold. She immediately recognized the coins, her mind flashing with the images she had seen only days ago.

"Isn't that some of the gold from the abandoned kingdom?" She whispered in Maverick's ear, her question answered with the simple nod of a head.

"I'm sorry, I left in such a hurry I forgot to bring gold," Maverick mumbled. "Besides, there was no one there to miss it, was there?" Celestia sighed, glaring in Maverick's direction. She couldn't help but feel uncomfortable, it was almost as if Maverick had stolen objects from a graveyard.

The shopkeeper, mouth agape and eyes wide, eyed the gold greedily. He thankfully pocketed the money, unaware of its true significance, and flashed a toothless smile as he dropped the coins into his apron.

"Are there any places we could change and possibly stay the night?" asked Maverick, the cashier hesitantly nodding his head in response.

"There's an inn down the street to the left. It's the only inn in town! I'm afraid it's not very orderly, but the service is pretty cheap, so if you're looking for somewhere to stay then that's the place."

Maverick nodded thankfully, placing their purchases into their new satchel. He then took the satchel in his own arms and turned to leave, Celestia following behind.

Maverick flung open the door and he and Celestia stumbled out into the cold once more. Celestia's feet immediately froze and Maverick's face was rosy. As they began walking once more, Celestia felt eyes boring into her back.

She turned quickly around, but no one was there.

Chapter 19

The snow began its gentle fall from the clouds, covering the path in a powdery white and sucking at the, now covered, feet of the two siblings. The street was quiet and the silence made Celestia feel uneasy. She wondered why everyone had hidden themselves, and wished they hadn't. She'd much rather be surrounded by laughter and voices than silence and eyes. Prying eyes, she noted.

A few people walked down the street. Celestia tried to draw their attention, but they ignored her presence and kept walking. Celestia glared ahead of her, feeling anger begin its slow burn.

Celestia was pulled from her irritated state as she crashed into Maverick and fell to the ground, her attention drawn to him. Celestia almost redirected her anger toward Maverick, but stopped.

She lifted herself up, following the sound of loud, disrespectful voices, awfully rowdy singing and the banging of beer steins. Her feet unknowingly led her to the front of a large, wooden building and the sound, much louder now, willed her to glance up. It was the Inn (and bar) that the cashier had mentioned! Maverick dragged himself up the creaking steps and pushed open the door, leaving the freezing cold behind him. Celestia stumbled in afterward. People were laughing and chatting, clinking glasses of who-knows-what. Celestia and Maverick crept forward, hoping not to disturb the friendly atmosphere.

Maverick held his breath, stepping cautiously on the floorboards. A loud creak sounded from beneath his foot, echoing through the whole room. The bar seemed to hold its breath, deathly quiet. Celestia and Maverick stood still, hoping they could go unnoticed. All eyes veered towards them. Maverick felt his lungs deflate.

"Sorry, just keep doing whatever you were doing before," stated Maverick, acting as though he was completely unaware of all the eyes trailing them. Maverick gripped Celestia's arm, his heart thundering in his ears and his palms sweaty. He stood straight and tall, but the prince was terrified. He was immediately thankful Celestia was there. Her presence calmed him, just a little, and he took on her same stance.

As soon as they reached the bar the silence broke and the excessive chattering started once more. "Never apologize in a bar full of delinquents." A hushed voice whispered. The siblings turned toward its owner. An old man stretched out on his stool before turning to face them.

"Noted." Celestia replied. The old man nodded, giving a toothless smile.

"What are ye doing in a place like this?"

"Looking for somewhere to change." Maverick answered plainly.

"We've traveled for quite some time and will also need a place to rest and, perhaps, have some dinner as well," Celestia finished. The old man nodded, his smile ever present.

"Then ye are talking to the right guy. Follow me." He croaked, standing from his stool and gripping the edge of the bar counter. He straightened himself and continued forward. People gave them sideward glances, but allowed them to pass.

Celestia and Maverick shuffled alongside the man, careful not to bump into people or crash into tables. The old man led them behind the counter and into a crevice in the wall. They entered a hallway, the noise immediately stopping. The man gestured upstairs.

"I'll be showing you to your room. It'll cost you, though." The distant clink of pans could be heard, drowning out the old man's brittle, worn voice. The softness to his voice made him seem more fragile than he wanted to appear. There was a bit of brokenness and secrecy in this man that Celestia could relate to, but she made no mention of it.

"Will this do?" Maverick asked, reaching into his pouch and plucking out one gold coin.

"This is more than enough!" the man exclaimed, cannily reaching for the gold. Maverick retracted his hand, shaking his head.

"This gold can be yours, but only if we're given a room, a warm bath, and two hot meals: dinner and breakfast." Maverick declared. The old man smiled in response, his watery eyes crinkling good-naturedly at the corners. He seemed to be getting more joy from his encounter with the siblings than he had felt in a long time.

"You drive a hard bargain, mister. But I suppose I'll have to settle!" The owner outstretched his hand and Maverick relinquished the gold piece.

"Nice dealing with you," said the old man as he jumped ahead of them, slowly making his way up the rickety stairs. Maverick and Celestia followed after him in single file; the stairs were fairly narrow. Maverick stumbled, landing on a cracked stair and watching as it fell apart.

"Aren't these dangerous?" Celestia asked, skeptically as she helped Maverick jump over the gap. The old man merely grunted in response.

Celestia felt the urge to continue conversing with the old man, and so she asked "Why are the people here so unfriendly? When we arrived here, we hardly saw anyone on the streets. Those that we did see immediately barricaded themselves in their houses."

The old man looked back at her as he continued climbing the staircase.

"When I was younger, this village was much friendlier and livelier, having no concerns and being able to find joy in everything. A couple decades ago, a dark beast appeared, lurking along the streets of the town but never approaching anyone. Even so, just the sight of the creature sent everyone fearfully retreating to their homes; they became so afraid of the beast that they mostly kept to themselves in their homes. The people here have learned to dread change and the unknown and have forgotten what it was like to live freely and worriless."

Celestia wondered what the dark beast looked like. Why were these people so scared of something they had only seen, when it hadn't done anything to harm them? That question churned in her mind and, although she wished to voice her question, she decided to keep it to herself.

When they finally reached the top of the stairs, the old man led them down a narrow hallway, stopping near the end and knocking on a door, the sound echoing back. He dug around in his back pocket for a few moments before pulling out a fat, rusty little key that fit snugly in the palm of his hand. Turning towards the two of them, he threw them their key, Celestia catching it mid air.

"It's not the most tidy of rooms, but I hope you enjoy your stay. I'll send one of my bartenders up with some food, so be expecting a knock on the door... If it doesn't fall down first." the old man stated laughingly, lightening the mood. Sidestepping his guests, the man hurried away, his footsteps fading as he moved back down the hallway and, with a final clatter, he was gone.

"How odd..." Maverick whispered. Celestia blinked, once, twice, struggling to comprehend what she and her brother had witnessed; she could recall nothing but the pain in the old man's voice when he was speaking of his own people.

Maverick, who thought nothing more of the old man's words about the beast, was the first to break their trance-like state. He stepped forward, thrusting the key into the lock and giving the doorknob a turn.

The door unlocked with a click. Maverick pushed it open, the hinges responding with a loud creak. He carefully entered the room, as a wary Celestia followed closely behind.

The floor groaned under the extra pressure, but still managed to stay intact. Although it wasn't worth even half of what they paid, it would have to do.

Two unframed mattresses rested on the floor in front of them, along with two rag blankets at the edge of each bed. The sheets were tangled and hanging half off the mattresses, almost as if the previous occupants had just barely left. The pillows were grimy and spotted with stains, and a glass lantern flickered, illuminating the dark and windowless room.

Celestia threw their satchel onto one of the mattresses. She pushed open a door beside their disgusting bedding and cringed as it creaked, revealing a fairly large, but very empty closet. Well, almost empty. Her eyes immediately dropped to a couple of twitching, fuzzy rats on the floor. Their red eyes seemed to fix on her, and she quickly shoved the door closed with a shiver of distaste. Nothing haunted her more than eyes, no matter what they belonged to. They always told secrets she'd rather not know.

This place was most definitely not a place for royalty, and it sickened Maverick. He could taste bile in his throat. Was this really how his people lived? Filthy, used bed sheets and mildew growing on their pillows? He felt a wave of sympathy before the nausea returned. As soon as they got back home he would have to make sure something was done about this in his own kingdom.

Maverick shut the door behind him, placing the key on a rickety table near the wall and gingerly stepping forward, hoping the floor wouldn't cave in. When it didn't, he was finally able to relax.

Hearing a curt knock coming from the door, Maverick hurriedly opened it, greeted with two hot bowls of stew and a loaf of bread by his feet. He grabbed the food eagerly, shutting the door promptly behind him. Maverick handed Celestia a bowl of stew and half of the loaf of bread. The siblings hungrily stuffed their faces full of sustenance, their empty stomachs grumbling in gratitude. Once they finished their dinner, they placed their empty dishes and utensils on the wobbly table. They took turns changing in the smelly closet before finally collapsing onto the mattresses to try to get a little rest.

Celestia's thoughts finally had the time to tiptoe back into her mind. Every time she closed her eyes all she could see was that pile of snow and Stars chest gently halting its movement. She thought of the stars in the heavens, and how as the life drained from her very own Star, one of the brightest stars in the sky seemed to blink out as well. She glanced at her brother for comfort, but he had already fallen asleep. She almost awoke him but stopped herself. She couldn't.

Sometimes, a burden was meant to be carried alone. And Maverick's snores were truly the only satisfactory thing Celestia needed at the moment. They reminded her profoundly that she was not alone; for now that was enough.

Celestia forced herself into a dreamless slumber, depression clawing at her mind as the night zoomed by.

Chapter 20

Celestia was used to taking care of herself, having lived in the tower alone all those years, and had come to appreciate how pleasant it was to keep her surroundings neat and clean. Skillfully, she made her bed in a matter of seconds, making the crusty sheets seem luxurious. Turning her head, she studied Maverick's awkward attempts to fold the sheets correctly on his mattress. He looked helplessly at Celestia, who scoffed.

"I understand that you've always had servants to do everything for you, but I am not your servant; you're going to need to learn to do things for yourself... starting with making your own bed." Celestia commented teasingly. Shaking her head, she wondered how Maverick had made it this far on his own when he could barely fold a blanket.

After many failed attempts, Maverick had finally managed to sloppily fold the sheets on his bed. Annoyed, Celestia fixed his bedsheets by simply tugging the corner, and then proceeded to place her belongings neatly in the satchel lying on her mattress. The siblings scurried around one another, readying themselves and the room for their departure. After tidying it up, the room looked much better than when they had first arrived.

Grabbing their new satchel, Celestia unlocked the door; she and Maverick stepped into the hallway. She didn't even bother to lock the door behind her, as there wasn't a point to secure something so barren. She slipped the key into her pocket and they made their descent down the stairs.

The stairs creaked with each step, causing the both of them to flinch. They avoided the chipped and broken wood, skidding down the rest of the way until they finally reached the bottom. With a sigh of relief, they walked out of the hallway and into the lounge, which was once again filled with people and loud voices but wasn't nearly as crowded as the evening before.

Celestia walked over to the bartender, who had already prepared seats for the both of them, steaming pots of chunky porridge sitting atop the long wooden bar. Celestia hurriedly swung onto a stool and Maverick followed uneasily after her. With a nod of the bartender's head, they dug in. Maverick was hesitant at first, but after realizing he had been surviving on nothing but stale bread, tough jerky, and sour berries the past few weeks he happily gulped down two bowls of the thick, hot gruel in no time at all.

Once Celestia had finished her third bowl, she settled back with a satisfied sigh and waited for Maverick to finish what was now his fifth.

"Where's the old man?" she questioned the bartender, cocking an eyebrow. She realized that she didn't even know his name, since he hadn't bothered to introduce himself. The bartender, who was polishing a glass, shrugged before turning to place the glass on the counter behind him.

"If it's the owner of this establishment you're referring to, his name is Heth." said the bartender. "And he's probably off gambling in a corner." The bartender leaned across the bar and lowered his voice so as not to be overheard.

"I'd be careful associating yourself with such a man," he said quietly, glancing about as he picked up another glass to polish.

Celestia nodded hesitantly, wondering why the bartender would be warning her about his employer, but deciding to take advantage of his helpfulness to find out more about the mysteries that lay within this town and its people.

"Heth mentioned last night that there is some sort of beast around? What kind of beast is it? Why are all so afraid of it?" The question seemed to catch the bartender off guard for the slightest moment, and his eyes roamed nervously over the room before he leaned forward.

"It's hard to describe it," stated the bartender, his voice quivering with suppressed fear. "It's like a mass of shadows that roams our streets. It always appears unexpectedly, but there is always a distinct chill in the air, almost like a fog descending, right before it appears. The people have grown so accustomed to this chilly feeling that they've developed a sixth sense that allows them to hide before it arrives," the bartender said with a knowing nod of his head before continuing. "Fear of this creature has overcome many residents of this town and gets in the way of many of our daily activities; it's the only thing that seems to be on most people's minds. I've never seen it personally because my parents trained me to know when to hide before it arrives, but I know that Heth has. He knows more than I do, so if you have any more questions just ask him."

Celestia's thoughts flashed back to the apparition that had been chasing them just before Star had collapsed and passed on. She knew exactly what creature the bartender was speaking of. Afraid he had been overheard, the bartender disappeared behind a door with a curt nod of his head.

Before he could ask for a sixth serving, Celestia whisked Maverick off his barstool and into the bustling crowd once more. She gripped his sweaty hand in her own, dragging him behind her as if she was leading a lost puppy.

Celestia wove through clumps of people, searching for the only familiar face that she knew. She caught a glimpse of the short tufts of greying hair and dragged Maverick forward, before stopping to tap Heth on the back. He turned and smiled cheerfully at the two.

"If it isn't my most recent customers! How did you sleep?" He exclaimed, squinting his eyes- which held the same mysterious glint they had the day before.

Celestia snorted, placing the rusty key in the man's outstretched hand. "We slept as well as possible in that filthy, rat infested room."

Heth stepped back, obviously offended by Celestia's remark, and defensively responded "Well, we do the best we can here, under the circumstances..."

"You mean, because of the beast?" Celestia inquired. "What is so frightening about that creature?"

Heth paused, his eyes flickering to and fro as though paranoid. A few prying eyes had settled on the three of them, standing still and silent in a mass of moving bodies. Heth leaned forward, only a breath away from Celestia's ear.

"*It* kills anyone who stands in its path, freezing them to the core. Some say that entire villages have fallen to its wrath centuries ago, and *it* won't stop haunting our village until every last living creature in its presence has been diminished. Some people haven't stepped outside their house in years, and others come here to drink away their terror. Don't let fear overcome you, my dear, or you'll become just like us." Heth paused, backing away and giving Celestia one last, firm glance and then disappearing into the crowd, dismissing the conversation. After a minute of regaining their composure and pondering the old man's words, Celestia turned around, pulling Maverick after her.

They finally stepped out of the stuffy atmosphere and into the chilly air. The snow crunched beneath their boots, making a path for the both of them.

Maverick nudged Celestia, pulling her from her silent reverie. With their new clothing, they fit right in with the townsfolk. The townsfolk, in turn, found them unthreatening and the people sat on their porches, chatting and laughing as their children chased each other through the snow.

Celestia stopped walking, watching as a little girl tripped, scraping her knee on the ice. Celestia stepped forward to help her, but never got the chance. The little girl's older brother and mother swooped down from the porch, pulling her into an embrace and comforting the little girl. Celestia looked away, a small smile etched across her face. She quickened her pace to join Maverick.

Suddenly, the whole world seemed to stop. Everyone froze, eyes wide with fear, as if they could sense something Celestia couldn't. Everyone rushed back into their homes, slamming and locking their doors behind them. In a matter of seconds, the whole town was quiet. Even the bar seemed to hold its breath. Celestia could feel the familiar bone chilling coldness seep through her skin. She slowly turned around.

That's when she saw *it*.

Chapter 21

Celestia could've sworn her heart was going to jump from her chest at any given moment. Luckily, it didn't.

It hovered falteringly at the end of the street, several yards away from the siblings. Although it had no eyes, only two empty sockets where they should've been, *it* seemed to be looking straight towards them. The black, smokey mass continually expanded and deflated as though it was breathing, gradually taking on the shape of an enormous wolf. *It's* teeth pulled into a snarling, unfaltering smile, plastered on its face. *It* may not have had eyes... but *it* clearly sensed Celestia and Maverick were there. It's head tilted at even the slightest, shallowest breaths either of the siblings released.

Maverick slowly backed up, snow crunching loudly underneath his boots. The creature immediately snapped toward him, causing him to let out a small shriek. Instantly, legs stretched out of the smoky mass and the creature sprung onto the ground. Celestia watched as *it* turned into an eyeless, snarling wolf, made completely of the cloudy black essence. *It's* tail lashed back and forth eagerly; now *it* knew they were there.

That's when Maverick ran. Celestia, turning, was hot on his heels. The beast leapt forward and bolted after both of them. Celestia hoped she wouldn't lose sight of her brother and, preferably, not be eaten.

Celestia couldn't help turning to look back, recognizing the creature's ghoulish grin and fumy fur; it was the same creature that had chased them through the forest with Star. A cold sense of dread overwhelmed her and her heart pounded deafeningly as the creature seemed to gain on them. The snow seemed to drag at their feet, slowing them down, but they forced themselves forward.

They twisted in and out of houses, not daring to stop for a breath. Celestia suddenly noticed the tailor shop they had first visited when stepping into the town. She veered towards the store, Maverick sensing and copying her movements. They raced towards the door, jumping onto the porch and pounding the wood furiously while trying to catch their breath. While they seemed to have lost the creature temporarily, Celestia knew *it* was somewhere close. She could sense *it* as her skin crawled with goosebumps, shivers running up and down her spine.

Maverick frantically reached past Celestia, jiggling the doorknob, but to no avail. In fact, Celestia swore she could hear muffled laughter from within, but there was no time to plead with the figure behind the door.

With one final curse and a well-aimed kick at the door, Maverick turned and bolted from the porch, shouting to his sister, "Run!" Celestia, filled with a sense of terror and alarm, turned blindly to follow her brother, and ran straight through the floating black mass that hovered silently behind her... and out the other side.

She felt as though her blood had literally run cold, filled with the ice of a million arctic tundras. It was a worse cold than anything she'd ever known, and she found herself literally frozen in place until Maverick grabbed her arm and started dragging her further away from the pulsating black mass that continued to hover at the bottom of the steps. Even when her limbs were no longer stiff, her breaths still came out in little puffs of smoke, her insides still chilled inhumanly. Her teeth chattered, her limbs shaking violently. Maverick knew that he needed to get Celestia away from the creature, for another swipe through that mass of cold and Celestia would be done for.

The mass had turned by then and followed them, slowly this time. As though stalking prey; taunting them.

Maverick raced from building to building, dragging a stumbling Celestia with him, pounding on each door and praying that someone would let them in. Although they could hear voices from within each house, their pleas were ignored. And yet the beast continued to follow them, slowly, deliberately, not letting them out of his sight, but not trying to attack then either.

Celestia was slowly regaining her senses after her encounter with the beast. She knew the townspeople were terrified of the creature, which had been taunting them and terrorizing the village for quite some time, so she understood why the villagers were unwilling to help them. They were afraid to risk even opening a door, for even a moment, because they would put themselves at risk. But as Celestia and Maverick stumbled about, trying best to avoid the slow phantom creeping behind them, she suddenly realized something the townspeople would have never known.

If they were truly in danger, Abaven would have been there by then. Even at the risk of being seen by the townspeople, Abaven would never have let Celestia come to any harm.

As they approached the edge of the village Celestia quickly skidded to a stop, pulling her arm from Maverick's desperate grasp. Maverick, panicking, reached to grab her hand again, yelling at her to keep running.

"Stop." Celestia ordered. Her voice was hushed and yet commanding. Maverick instantly skidded to a stop, turning to look at Celestia questioningly, which was when he realized that the order wasn't directed toward him.

The black beast had also stopped, its vicious snarl turning into a lopsided grin, almost as though it was amused. Celestia felt as though *it* was staring at her, as if *it* was waiting for something.

Celestia stood completely still, fighting against her every instinct and slowing her breathing, allowing her heart to completely control her actions. Even she was amazed as her hand extended and her fingers reached forward to touch the cool surface of the beast's skin. An immediate chill flowed through her fingertips, but still she stepped forward. The black mass stopped shifting, taking on a solid form and allowing her to stroke *it's* snout. The beast gently pressed *it's* snout into her hand, as if *it* wanted her to continue stroking *it*. Slowly, she could sense a bond forming between them and she could tell the creature wanted to share something with her.

As Celestia looked around, she spotted villagers staring from their windows, gasping and whispering. She felt a wave of sweet defiance washing over her. The shadowy beast never wanted to cause them harm; the villagers were terrified of *it* because they never tried to understand it. And while Celestia wanted to remove her hand and call the people out on their mistaken assumptions...

The *memories* came before she had the chance to. As she stroked its snout, its memories began to transfer to her, flowing through her mind with increasing speed. It took all of Celestia's strength to withstand the torturous flashbacks and recollections of the creature's past. All it had ever known was fear and terror towards people, because they were always trying to harm him. She could picture the creature pursuing others in loneliness and scaring them.

When they would lash out at it, the beast would freeze them in self defense. Flashes of crumbling buildings and screaming people marched through her mind while blood and death accompanied. Thousands of hateful eyes and abusive hands were directed toward the beast, filling him with agonizing sensations of desolation and guilt.

The creature's memories twisted in and out of her thoughts, the years of endless anguish now on the princess's shoulders.

And then came the day it first sensed Celestia and Maverick.

Although it couldn't see them, at first, the creature could feel a special bond between the siblings. As this feeling of love and friendship grew between them, the creature began to see Maverick and Celestia. For the first time since the beginning of its existence, the beast could actually see people and their interactions with each other, and it desired to befriend them.

The creature followed the sound of footsteps through the woods. It was fascinated by the laughter that emitted from their mouths and the love that danced in their eyes. It was entranced by the irreplaceable bond the two... no... three figures had.

Although it couldn't see them, at first, the creature could feel a special bond between the siblings. As this feeling of love and friendship grew between them, Maverick, Celestia, and Star slowly became visible to the creature. For the first time since the beginning of its existence, the beast could actually see people and their interactions with each other, and it desired to befriend them.

And so It kept following them. It followed them like a dog being led by biscuit treats. Like a cat following a trail of catnip. It didn't want to eat them, it didn't want to devour them, or harm them, or do anything other than withhold even the tiniest fraction of the unbreakable bond they seemed to share. It was lonely, and all it wanted was company. Friends. Someone to share it's smile-free life with.

Finally, the beast gathered up the courage to show itself unto them. But as it neared them, they ran away. The beast couldn't do anything but watch as their figures disappeared and listen to the raging clips of horse feet and scared, rigid breaths of more people running away.

Sulking back into the shadows, the poor creature thought of what it could have. Of the little fantasy that it could only dream of. It was naive to believe it could ever be worthy of anything other than loneliness.

Celestia knew that while she had misjudged the creature, the entire kingdom had as well. The poor creature had known nothing but fear and terror, and had never meant to cause those feelings in others. All it wanted was to be accepted and welcomed.

Suddenly the creature, the feared beast, became not a threat, but a being and a presence. And Celestia understood. *It* had shown her, clearly, that people scare themselves silly, even when there is nothing to fear.

Just as she had, those many years in the tower, afraid of the world outside of it.

Celestia removed her hand, her heart drumming in rhythm with the beast's. She felt her knees buckle, and she dropped to the ground. That was when she noticed the white orb, strumming and pulsating in the midst of the black mass. It seemed to call out to her, begging her and pleading her to free it from the shadows that encased it. Her eyes seemed drawn to the orb. It was entrancing, the way the shadows rolled over it as though they could not fully engulf it. The way the brightness of the orb never dulled, no matter how thick the shadows became.

The creature settled down next to Celestia and laid its head in her lap. Once again, the creature began to take the solid form of a wolf as it relaxed, and Celestia gently stroked its smokey fur. The wolf's eyelids fluttered closed, momentarily blocking out those two vacant eye sockets. The creature sighed deeply, then opened and revealed two golden-hued eyes that gazed up at Celestia with complete trust. Her breath hitched in her throat as she gazed into the eyes of her new friend. The white orb at the creature's center began pulsating more brightly, seeming to call out to Celestia as she locked gazes with the wolf. Suddenly, she knew exactly what she had to do.

Celestia sucked in a deep breath and reached her hand through the shadowy mat of fur. Cold pricked her skin, but despite the chills she continued reaching. She knew that this final act would set the creature free. She would be able to end the misery, guilt and loneliness that was all the creature had ever known. She could show it love and could finally give it what it longed for all along. A friend.

As soon as her fingers grazed the white orb at the beast's center, her whole body was filled with an overwhelming wave of heat. Her shivers stopped, her blood pumping with warmth once more. The black smoke of the creature began to disperse and it gave Celestia one last smile before disappearing in a flash of light. The smoke swirled into the white orb, which Celestia grasped firmly in her hand. She carefully stroked the orb and felt a small tear trickle down her cheek.

She could've sat there for hours, just looking into the orb and listening to its indecipherable whispers, but Maverick pulled her to her feet and broke her from her trance. After a few seconds of staring into the empty space where the creature had been, Celestia knew it was time to move forward. She carefully placed the orb in her satchel and turned to walk back into the village, Maverick falling into step beside her.

People slowly trickled out of their homes, smiling in relief and laughing. Snowflakes fell, confetti to the people's lost fear. They danced through the streets, crying with glee. Some even glanced at the glowing bag. Celestia inhaled sharply, trying to ignore the people's movements. Maybe they'd learn to live again.

But they weren't the ones who had been saved.

Chapter 22

Celestia continuously fingered the white orb that lay glittering in her satchel. It seemed to draw her towards it, as though they had been separated for far too long, and were finally reunited. Despite its consistent calls for her, she simply savored the warmth that it emitted, sitting on the porch of the inn. Maverick sat down beside her.

"How do you suppose we're going to get home?" Maverick questioned, his eyes nervously flickering to the orb that was now balanced between Celestia's hands. Celestia shrugged, staring sadly into the orb and ignoring the laughter and freed voices ringing throughout the village.

"We have no horses... and it would be unsafe to ride Abaven for too long," She said shortly, staring skyward thoughtfully. She could still feel the slight stinging sensation in her heart, a reminder that Star was gone. Maverick sighed, nodding his head.

"Another trek on foot then, I suppose?" he inquired, his breath already ragged just thinking of how exhausted he'd be after another week of constant walking and trudging through the elements.

Once the two rose from the porch, deciding it was finally time for their departure, they noticed the crowd of villagers surrounding the inn, chatting and giggling and playing amongst themselves. Their behavior was alien compared to the way they acted before.

Two men and a woman stepped out from the crowd.

"Thank you." The woman smiled, pulling Celestia into an unexpected embrace. The woman stepped back, tears streaming down her cheeks.

"Sorry." She sniffed, wiping away her tears.

"You saved us. We don't have to live in fear any longer. We don't have to be afraid anymore!" she acknowledged. Everyone was smiling and cheering in the siblings direction. Their eyes shone with pure admiration.

"I didn't save you all," Celestia began, watching as the villagers' smiles turned lopsided in confusion.

"I proved to you all that your fears were based on your own prejudices. I hope that, from now on, you're able to take the time to learn about others before you judge them. You scared yourselves silly over a creature that, in reality, only wanted some company. He hadn't meant to hurt you at all," Celestia finished, watching as the villagers' facial expressions twisted shamefully.

"You're right," the lady whispered regretfully. Many of the other villagers nodded and mumbled in response.

"We were wrong about the creature, and we were wrong about you. Thank you for teaching us that. You have to let us repay you in some way! The least we can do is give you protection." The woman turned toward the two men.

"This is Ralf and Eugene." She gestured toward the men that accompanied her. They each smiled in turn, and Celestia beamed. Maverick glared suspiciously at the two and, taking notice of his frown and scowl, Celestia elbowed her brother, causing him to wince and force a small smile.

"Actually," Celestia started, thinking back to Abaven and how she longed to feel the air whooshing past her once more, without supposedly falling to her death.

"We don't exactly need protection, but there is something we desperately need at the time. Is there any way you'd be willing to make us something instead?" Celestia asked, Maverick's eyes lighting up immediately. He knew exactly what she wanted to ask for, and had decided he wanted it just as badly. Anything would be better than walking and trekking through the snow all the way home.

"Anything, we owe so much to you," The lady bowed, the citizens bowing with her.

"No need for that!" Celestia yelped, the people straightening apologetically, as though they had just offended their savior. Celestia stared questioningly at these people. She found it interesting that the same people who would not open their doors to her just moments ago, now were willing to bow to her.

"Is there any way you can make a horse saddle... but around 20x its normal size? Like, within the next few hours?" Maverick piped in, a chortle of a laugh bubbling in his throat. He knew their answer would be no, but it was worth a try. The question seemed absolutely ridiculous.

"Are you sure? Don't you just want a normal saddle?" The lady asked, seemingly taken aback.

"Or an unusually large and strong cloth will do, too." Celestia piped in, becoming aware of how unexplainably challenging her request actually was. The lady seemed relieved at her possible alternative and sent off Ralph and Eugene - who disappeared into the crowd at her words. Dozens of people began to disperse, all heading in the same direction, towards the tailor's store at the corner of the town. They all seemed to pick up more people along the way, and suddenly the whole crowd had disappeared, all retreating towards that small shop.

The lady started in their direction, too.

"We'll be right back," She called, skidding through the snow in the direction of the others.

Celestia and Maverick erupted into a chorus of laughter, both staring in the direction the townspeople had disappeared and wondering just why they accepted such a hard task. How, they wondered, had they gotten so lucky as to have the chance to go through the rest of their journey upon the back of a dragon?

It only seemed like a matter of seconds before the crowd emerged from the little abode once more, dispersing to make room for both Ralph and Eugene. Both men progressed forward, carrying a giant piece of fabric between each other.

"A ship's captain had ordered this large piece of canvas as a new sail for his ship, but he has never returned to retrieve it. Will this do?" Celestia could tell the fabric was thick and sewn together nicely, and so she nodded her head in response.

The lady guided Ralph and Eugene, and all of the townspeople followed after her. A line of citizens followed the two men carrying the blanket, just watching and waiting, as if they expected them to drop it.

They hauled the fabric into the hands of Celestia and Maverick immediately upon reaching them, huffing deeply, showing their effort in moving their massive creation.

"Do you need help carrying it to your destination?" The lady asked after pausing for a deep breath.

Celestia and Maverick shook their heads, heaving the fabric between them. It was indeed heavy, but nothing they couldn't manage.

"Thank you so much," Celestia sighed, giving them a small, sheepish smile. Person after person nodded, the lady embracing Celestia once more. Celestia wiggled from her tight grip, watching as the lady wiped away tears of joy.

"No, thank you. You have no idea how long.." The lady disappeared into the crowd, choking back sobs. People poured from their homes, adding to the crowd around the siblings. They smiled and cheered. Celestia searched the crowd, finding the family she had spotted only a day before. The little girl smiled at her and waved. Celestia smiled back, fixing the fabric in her arms and, in sync with Maverick, started trudging forward.

"Actually," Celestia stopped for a moment, immediately catching the attention of the crowd behind her.

"Follow us, there's something else we would like to show you." Maverick looked quizzically at Celestia, but she just smiled in response. 'Trust me,' she seemed to say.

The townsfolk followed closely behind the siblings until they had made it a safe distance from the village. Celestia ordered the villagers to back up and then raised two fingers to her lips and let out a long, deafening whistle.

The flap of wings could be heard, clouds of white snow lifting from the ground and covering the siblings and the villagers. Many people screamed, a few ran, but a couple of people had remembered

Celestia's words and chose not to be overcome with fear from the beast.

The crowd watched the large beast land, his giant, scaly feet creating large, abnormal footprints in the snow. Celestia lunged forward with Maverick in tow, and embraced the snout of her beast.

"He's not something to be frightened of," Celestia shouted, beckoning the villagers towards her. "Come, pet him, he won't bite!"

The first person to step forward was the little girl and her older brother, who hesitantly stroked the scales of her beast. Smiles sprung onto their faces as they realized he was not something to be feared. Abaven's mouth pulled into a toothy grin, and he nuzzled the little girl with his snout. At the sound of her giggle, many of the other townspeople stepped forward, carefully stroking Abaven and coming to the realization that appearance doesn't always determine character.

Abaven lay down in the snow and, after a few more moments, many of the townsfolk backed up while Ralph and Eugene helped to fasten and secure the fabric on Abavens back. The two siblings climbed up his wing, carefully seating themselves atop their improvised dragon-saddle.

Finally, staring out at the villagers below them and the mountains behind them, Celestia felt relieved. She knew Abaven wouldn't be harmed by any villagers, with the added bonus of secured seating.

Once Abaven started moving his wings, Celestia found herself lifted off the ground, staring down at specks of wonder-struck townsfolk and tiny wooden abodes and shops. Maverick hurriedly clung to her, scared out of his wits.

But even so, the wind against her skin, the beautiful clouds rushing past them, the pure white canvas beneath them; those were all things she would never forget. Things that cleared her of her troubles for the time being.

And, looking at Maverick, Celestia realized he felt the same way and thought the exact same thoughts. And for the time being, nothing else mattered. Celestia was ready for whatever came next.

She'd be brave or she'd fall. And she wasn't ready to fall just yet.

Chapter 23

The journey, which should have taken days, was over in just a few hours, and as the castle became visible below them Celestia found anxiety beginning to bubble in her stomach. She had absolutely no idea what this next experience would be like.

Once it became clear that the large castle from her imagination was actually small and humble, and that the entire kingdom was actually quite welcoming, she found herself able to relax. It was nothing as she had remembered but it was, in fact, even better. The anxiety that had been clawing at her stomach for the entirety of the journey had finally dissipated, almost entirely. No more knots twisted in her stomach, and her heart no longer felt as though it was made of lead. She could finally breathe without the intolerant presence of fear at her side. And although she still felt nerves twisting in her stomach, she knew she would be fine. It was a beautiful feeling that she relished completely; a feeling of sweet relief.

Once Abaven had landed a good, safe distance away from the prying eyes of villagers, Celestia found herself slipping off his scaly, bumpy wings and planting her feet on the ground below. It felt almost surreal, touching the soil of her former kingdom and thinking of the little speck of hideous tower that had made her miserable for so long; now miles and miles behind them. Maverick could see it too and, as soon as he was on his feet again, he made sure to place a hand on Celestia's shoulder.

She had become so much more without those tower walls to confine her.

And when Maverick looked at her, he found himself surprised. He had only known her for a few weeks, and yet all he could feel was love. For this stranger who magically happened to be his sister, and a love that said he cared for her. Even if he knew almost nothing about her, Maverick would lay down his life, his last breath, to save her own. To conserve her last breath for a later time. His love for his older sister was unfathomable.

As Abaven growled his last goodbye before departing, Celestia too realized how much she loved both Abaven and Maverick. She could feel Abaven nudge her with his snout, and kissed his inky black scales in parting. Her heart had never felt so much joy just being in the presence of those two beings, and just glancing in their direction calmed the shreds of angst that longed to build itself up and take direction of Celestia's actions. And soon, her family would be complete.

Celestia gazed to her side, half expecting Abaven to be there but just barely realizing he had gone. She could see the quick shadow of him disappearing into the horizon, and Celestia knew it wouldn't be long until she'd see him again.

Even so, Celestia longed to whistle for him, to plead him to return, but she figured it wouldn't be the best idea while being so close to a village. Even if the people were the most noble of citizens, that wouldn't stop them from fearing something twenty times as large as them. It was too risky. Even Celestia had feared him, at one point! It had taken her years to warm up to the idea of him.

And although Celestia was fully open to taking risks, the safety of Abaven was much more important than that desire; she would not put him in peril.

She wished he could stay and stand by her side whilst she finally returned to the kingdom she had despised for so long. But instead, she reasoned, she would simply have to tell him all about it when she saw him again.

After a few promising words were exchanged between the two siblings, and Celestia had been reassured that Abaven would be alright, they turned toward the village and began walking along the dusty road. Celestia relished the dust clouding up with each step.

As soon as her feet touched the cobblestone pavement at the entrance of the village, her body turned rigid. She forced herself to move, gazing at each dwelling and taking in each feature as though she was moving into a new neighborhood. She felt a strange sense of deja vu clouding out all her other senses. Maverick tugged her forward, forcing her to keep pace with him. The bridge to the castle seemed to grow closer every second.

Suddenly, Celestia tripped, rolling onto the ground and scraping her knees. It took her a few seconds to process what had happened.

"I'm so sorry!" An old woman yelped, running over and helping Celestia to her feet. The woman fixed her shawl before rushing to pick up dozens of apples that had tumbled from her lopsided cart. Celestia joined in, picking up the bruised fruits and wiping them off. It didn't take them long to refill the cart. The woman huffed but wiped her filthy hands on her dusty skirt, smiling at Celestia.

"Thank you." The woman said, pushing her cart down the road and disappearing from Celestia's sight. Celestia hurried to catch up with her brother, who had stopped a few paces ahead and was studying the townsfolk. Their clothes were dusty and torn, their faces covered in dirt. But they were all helping each other; smiling, chatting and laughing together. Although Celestia's experience with people was limited, having spent so many years locked in the tower alone, she felt that these people were somehow special. She smiled, staring ahead and studying the castle from afar. She was immediately grateful. For her dragon. For her brother. And for the journey and finally making it to where she had desired to be all along. She had made it.

Little children danced too and fro, tumbling in front of Celestia. A little boy stumbled, Celestia quickly caught him and helped him to his feet.

"Thanks miss." The child smiled, his teeth uneven and missing. He sped off, joining the other children in their games. The mothers shouted to the younglings, calling them in for lunch as they hung clothes and bought vegetables and fruits from vendors. Celestia loved the liveliness and the welcoming hearts of the people. Maverick looked absolutely relieved to be with his people once more.

Dozens of villagers crowded the streets and cheered "Welcome home, prince Maverick!" He waved at each passing villager, smiling and exchanging brief conversations. The overjoyous claps of Maverick's subjects filled Celestia with a sense of acceptance, ridding her mind of daunting thoughts of the past.

Once the people finally began to quiet and retreat into their homes, Celestia nudged Maverick on the shoulder. "You'd be a good king someday. The people here seem to adore you." Maverick laughed.

"I'd hope so."

The two siblings linked arms, the noises in the village suddenly growing distant as they boarded the bridge. The stones glistened and shone beneath their feet. Celestia and Maverick twirled across the tiles, watching their reflections in the water below them and paying no heed to the villagers that could be watching.

Once they had made it halfway across the bridge, Maverick steadied Celestia, continuing forward in a more proper manner. He walked along the rest of the pavement gracefully, expecting Celestia to do the same. To Maverick, the tone was different, and something that needed to be respected. To him, these castle walls were holy, and upon approaching them he felt obligated to show his home the respect it deserved.

Celestia peered upward, the castle towering above them. It was terrifying, but beautiful. The guards standing next to the large, wooden castle doors took one glance at Maverick and promptly opened the gates. They patted him on the back as he walked in. Celestia followed afterward, the guards throwing her questioning glances from beneath their helmets. It only took them a few moments to realize the resemblance between her and Maverick. They quieted.

This would be a day the kingdom would never forget. *Everyone* could feel it. The guards, the servants, the villagers... and one shan't forget the king and queen.

Chapter 24

Celestia trailed her fingers along the castle's interior wall, following Maverick through it's maze-like halls. This was home. Maybe not her home, not yet, but it still seemed to embrace her from the moment she stepped inside.

The castle, Celestia was beginning to realize, was quite smaller than she remembered. It was more like a large house than a castle, holding no extra rooms, as everything held something or someone. There seemed to be a lack of staff, and the interior was crumbling to the extent she knew the stones hadn't been replaced in awhile .

In a way, the kingdom could easily crumble, yet she didn't know what held it together. The royal family, it seemed, were almost in as much poverty as the people.

Finally, the siblings reached a large set of doors, which towered over both of them. Guards who looked as though their armor had been crusted in a layer of rust for years, were stationed at each end.

Maverick leaned forward, whispering to both guards. The two moved, fiddling with the large doors. They slowly slid open, showing people huddled around a long table in a room that, to Celestia, was supposedly a miniscule ballroom.

Maverick took Celestia by the arm and led her directly to the table. The nobles and advisors rejoiced at the prince's presence and stood from the table immediately, crowding the siblings and fumbling with greetings. He avoided answering questions and replying to comments by waving his hand, stating "I would like to speak with the king and queen." At that statement, the nobles and advisors stepped aside and abruptly halted their chatter. Maverick strutted towards his parents, who were still sitting at the table and had just noticed his arrival. The queen pushed aside her chair, rising from the head of the table and rushing forward, enveloping Maverick in a warm embrace. Maverick scowled, untangling himself from her grasp. He glared at his parents in displeasure until he noticed the bewilderment on their faces. They didn't know.

"What are you wearing Maverick? Oh, no matter, we were so worried about you. Well, I was. Your father assured me you would be fine but.." The queen looked past Maverick, staring at Celestia quizzically. Celestia straightened her posture and gulped, struggling to stay in place while her mother studied her as if she were a total stranger. The king did the same. After several moments of awkward silence, Celestia cleared her throat. The queen slowly moved forward, stopping in front of Celestia and inspecting her as if she were a piece of art. Her jaw dropped in shock and tears sprung from her eyes.

"Oh my lord." The queen wheezed, gripping Celestia by the arms and staring into her eyes. The queen immediately saw the resemblance between Celestia and herself.

"Celestia... *Celestia?* Is that really you?"

Maverick placed an arm on Celestia's shoulder, yanking her from his mother's grasp.

"Yes! This is Celestia, the lost princess... and *my sister*! How could you have possibly kept her from me, all of these years? If you were keeping her in that tower to protect her, you failed. You failed to protect her from herself. From desperation and loneliness. Have you ever once thought of how it would affect *her*? *ME?*" he seethed.

The king stepped up from the table, placing himself beside his wife and gazing at the girl in front of them. He had known it was Celsetia from the moment she had walked through those doors, but his own guilt kept him from leaping up to greet her.

"There is a prince named Lucier, the son of the ruler of the South Eastern kingdoms, who wants to obtain all of the land in this region. He's asked many good kings and queens to hand over their kingdoms to him, but your mother and I are few of the rulers who refused. We knew that he craved power; he never intended to kindly rule over his subjects.

Lucier is a merciless tyrant who will kill anyone who disobeys him; he has burned many kingdoms into nothing more than ashes in order to seize their territory. After we refused his offer to rule our kingdom and allow us to peacefully part ways, he knew he would have to abide by the rules of our kingdom in order to obtain it.

When the kingdom was created, it was decreed that it pass from the king to his eldest child and has done so for centuries. It also states that if the king and queen do not have any children to pass the kingdom on to, then the entire kingdom reverts back to our large and powerful adjoining kingdom, Vestica - one that prince Lucier has no chance of taking over. Because Celestia is older than you,

Maverick, the throne would be inherited by her as soon as your mother and I passed on. Lucier knew that he could not kill us, or the kingdom would once more belong to Vestica. So his only chance of taking the throne would be to marry Celestia, automatically giving him rule over all of the kingdom's subjects and obtain the monocratic domination he desired; he would finally be considered a *king* and no longer a prince.

And so, to keep that from happening, we hid Celestia away, knowing full well that Lucier would never attempt to take our kingdom without our approval or marriage to our daughter. Over the years, Lucier has sent several troops in search of her, but he hasn't yet been able to find her. He has begged and pleaded with your mother and I for us to peacefully hand over the kingdom, but we will always refuse."

The king paused for a moment, trailing off as tears sprung to his eyes. When he gathered the courage to begin talking again, emotion was laced in his voice.

"I'm sorry that we've never had the courage to stand up to Lucier. Your mother and I have always feared what would become of the kingdom if Lucier became it's ruler, and that fear has caused us to choose our kingdom over our daughter. I'm sorry, Celestia, and I'm sorry Maverick."

Even though he was king, the emotions surging through him at that moment were too strong for him to suppress. His lip trembled, bitter tears of heartache and regret threatening to spill. The queen stepped forward, wrapping her arms around her husband. He quickly returned the embrace, sobbing wholeheartedly into her shoulder. Maverick felt the temporary hatred for his parents disintegrate into dust at his feet. Celestia grabbed Maverick's hand, looking into his eyes for a sense of reassurance, and together they joined in on the family hug.

"I forgive you." Celestia whispered. At those words, the king squeezed his family tighter to him. After a couple more moments holding them, he was first to break what seemed like an everlasting embrace. A look of seriousness washed over his face as he took Celestia's hands in his own.

"I know now that the tower is no longer an option, and I don't wish to keep you hidden any longer. Tomorrow, first thing in the morning, we must construct a plan to defeat Lucier once and for all. No longer will I choose my kingdom over my daughter. From now on, I choose both."

Chapter 25

Celestia was led to the unfamiliar bedroom of her childhood. She took in the flamboyant pink walls and dusty decorations, and felt oddly out of place. This wasn't her, and she didn't know how, no matter how young she had been, she had been able to stand any aspect of the room. The only part of the room that she didn't fully dislike was the windowsill, which actually held quite a spectacular view.

"I don't know how I never found this room," Maverick whispered, stepping in beside her. Both registered the unruly way that the fluffy, purple sheets hung oddly off the side of the bed, pillows were strewn all over the floor, and clothes lie untouched on top of a 3-legged dresser.

Just from the appearance, it became obvious that the room hadn't been touched since she had last been inside it. Rat droppings lined the floor, and Celestia spotted parts of the room she would pride herself in never drawing near.

"You know," Started Maverick, his eyes glazing over the disgusting scene of contention from so long ago.

"You could always just sleep in the guest room, which is actually right beside mine."

Celestia took no time to ponder Maverick's offer, agreeing without a moment's hesitation. He hurriedly led Celestia away from the nightmare of her childhood, which was closed off with the simple shutting of a door, and down the hallway towards his own quarters. It only took a few seconds to actually reach his bedroom, and he showed Celestia the room directly beside it.

The room she would be staying in was humble, blandly decorated, but nonetheless cozy. To Celestia, it was much more appealing than sleeping on the floor, or on unwashed mattresses and filthy pillows. This bedding, she figured, wouldn't be riddled with bed bugs, spiders, or ants.

After placing her meager number of possessions in the room, Maverick and Celestia spent their time in his room, which was quite large compared to the guest bedroom, held nice, cheap furniture (that looked expensive), and which had a fair arrangement of pristine princely apparel.

They talked of what the events of the next day would bring.

"I'm not ready to be king, I don't know if I'll ever be ready." Maverick said, honestly. Celestia shook her head.

"Maverick, I know it seems like a daunting title to hold, but based on what I have seen, your subjects already look up to you and admire you; they believe in you! I believe in you! You've been nothing but kind to me since the moment I've met you, and I've watched you grow to be extremely courageous. You will be a great leader and a wonderful king." Maverick smiled sheepishly, and Celestia could tell that he was holding back tears.

"Thank you, Celestia. I need you to know that whatever comes with tomorrow, I will be with you every step of the way, Celestia. I need you to know something..." Maverick hesitated, walking around the room and picking up a book. He flipped mindlessly through its pages before closing it and placing it back down again. Celestia waited, watching him. Finally, he took in a deep breath and summoned up the courage to look her in the eyes. Tears sparkled at the corners of his eyes and Celestia felt a tug at her heart. There was an unmistakable pain that rushed through her, seeing him like this, and it took every ounce of her strength, every single strand of will in her mind, not to run over to him and hug him.

Maverick needed this moment: one where he had to reassure himself he could survive, even without the suddenly all-too-comfortable presence of his older sister in the room.

"Even if I never spoke to you again, there wouldn't be a day that went by that I wouldn't be worrying about you. That I wouldn't think of you, and wish you could be there with me."

Celestia couldn't bring herself to respond, a lump forming in her throat that she knew would erupt into a series of sobs if she so much as opened her mouth. But Maverick seemed to read her thoughts without so much as an utterance of a single syllable.

"I love you, Celestia." He whispered, his lips forming a lopsided smile. Celestia nodded her head, willing herself to swallow the lump in her throat.

"I love you too, Maverick." Celestia wanted to say more. She wanted to tell Maverick to what extent she truly loved him. That she would give her life for his own, and that every moment she spent with him was another moment of forgotten loneliness.

But she knew he needed nothing more than the three worded response 'I Love You', and so she left it at that.

When the siblings finally stopped chatting, it was far past midnight, and Celestia returned to her temporary bedroom to ready herself for what the next day would bring. Readying herself to leave Maverick, to leave her newly found family.

But as soon as her body flopped against the mattress, she could hear a commotion in the distance, and felt immediate dread in the pit of her stomach. Something was definitely wrong.

Digging around in her satchel, she grabbed the bright, glowing orb and pulled it out. After a few seconds of watching the light dance in her hands and watching the shadows in her room move along with it, she stuffed it into a pocket in her trousers.

Ever since she had come in possession of the orb, she felt the need to keep it close to her at all times.

When Celestia twisted out of bed and opened the door, she could hear faint screams echoing through the walls of the castle and slowly growing louder. She could see the weaponed shadows of men dancing across the walls and hurried down the hallway to Maverick's door, knocking on it in alarm. She waited, but nobody answered. Celestia began pounding on the door, the shadows and voices growing closer.

"Come in," Maverick's hoarse voice was muffled and restrained, echoing from behind the door. She quickly swung the door open, closing it behind her as soon as she stepped inside. She spotted a lump underneath the blankets of the bed and stepped toward it.

"Maverick, someone's here." She whispered. The lump didn't budge. She crept closer, studying the lump.

"Maverick?" She questioned. The lump didn't move. She poked the lump, but received no movement in return. Eyeing the covers, she drew the blankets; only to find the lump was a pile of pillows.

"Celestia." A voice drawled. It wasn't her brother. She whipped around. There were six figures, veiled in shadows, pressed against the wall next to the door. The room was suddenly illuminated by light, she could see the figures clearly. One of the figures was Maverick. His eyes were blindfolded and a burly man held him, pressing a knife to his throat. Another man stepped forward.

His hair was as black as the shadows that had formerly encased him. His eyes were different colors. One blue and one yellow. He stroked the scruff along his chin and peered at the princess thoughtfully.

"You'd make a fine wife to my son. Isn't that right, Lucier?" A younger man, obviously the son, stepped forward. He cackled, his blue eyes gleaming and his white teeth flashing.

"Most definitely, father." Celestia couldn't move. Two men grabbed her arms from behind and dragged her to the door. She glanced from side to side, recognizing both of them immediately. They were the guards that had allowed Maverick and Celestia to enter the castle earlier that day. Celestia struggled against their grip, causing the strange-eyed man to glare in Celestia's direction.

It was awful to think that such treachery could come from the ones they had trusted only hours before. This was a sense of betrayal that was unbeknownst to Celestia before.

"If you so much as flinch we won't hesitate to sink this blade into your brother's neck." Celestia's eyes flickered toward Maverick. The blade scraped his skin, drawing tiny flecks of blood that dribbled down his neck and stained his collar. His breaths were ragged and his face was bruised.

Celestia quieted, allowing the men to lead her down the stairs of the palace and through the corridor. She peered into the open doors of the small ballroom as they passed by and immediately wished she hadn't. It was a bloodbath. The king's soldiers were lying on the floor, caked in their own blood and she caught a glimpse of her father among them. His sword was in his hand and his eyes were glazed; he lay in a pool of his own blood.

Celestia felt anger course through her; Lucier had cheated her out of the opportunity to get to know her father. Rage fizzled suddenly into sadness and she found herself reminiscing on the few, fleeting moments she remembered with him. Although she had never gotten to know him, she knew how deeply he had cared for her and Maverick and wished that he had more time.

Upon observing the battle scene more, Celestia managed to conclude that her mother wasn't amongst the dead and could only hope she was all right.

Maverick's blindfold was dotted in tear stains. He knew his father was no more. Celestia could only empathize, not knowing the full extent of Maverick's pain. She could only acknowledge that the relief she had felt when reuniting with her family once more was gone. It was taken from her with no chance of mercy and no opportunity for protest. Just like everything had been taken from her before.

The men continued dragging the two through the halls of the castle and deeper into the darkness. Finally they stopped. One of the men strode forward, opening a dark wooden door encased in shadows. Celestia could barely see where they were taking her, the area ahead of her nothing but a thick black mat of shadows. Her surroundings were blurry and unfocused, and the only comfort she had at the moment was the warmth of the orb in her pocket.

"Light the torches." One of the men called. Seconds later, the enormous staircase, winding downwards into the depths of the castle was fully illuminated, as bright as midday.

Celestia watched attentively as they guided her through stony hallways, taking note of the objects around her. If she were to escape, she needed to know how to get out of the maze of a castle. She turned a corner, carefully descending the stairway they led her down. The journey was silent, with the exception of the occasional profanity uttered by the men as they faltered on the stairs. Finally, Celestia stumbled over the last step and onto the ground. She opened her eyes, peering around.

The bright light of the torches had dimmed in the dank atmosphere and the floor was covered in rat droppings, decaying pieces of fruit, and murky puddles of what Celestia could only guess was urine. The temperature was a good fifteen degrees cooler, and everything seemed to leave her feeling cold.

They had arrived in the dungeon.

The men nudged Celestia with their feet, hauling her off the ground. As soon as she stood they pushed both her and Maverick forward, they placed a handkerchief over Celestia's mouth, causing her surroundings to blur and the world to spin.

The world went black.

Chapter 26

The first thing Celestia saw when she woke up was a rat. It scurried across the floor as soon as she stirred, disappearing beneath the bars of the shadowy cell. She blinked, her mind still foggy, her head pounding with each beat of her heart, and her surroundings nothing but a colorless backdrop. The floor beneath her was moist and cold, the stones dampened with either blood or tears (she couldn't quite tell in the dark). Celestia's hair was matted and disheveled, she constantly had to wipe loose strands of her golden locks from her eyes. Celestia struggled to push herself off the floor, but her legs failed her. Crumbling to a heap on the floor, Celestia could feel herself overcome with fear; with grief; with guilt.

"I'm sorry," Celestia wailed, pulling her knees to her chest as sobs racked through her body.

It was her fault Maverick was suffering, her fault her father had been killed and perhaps her mother as well, but she couldn't be certain. It was her fault the kingdom had been taken over, and her fault Star was no more. It was all her fault.

If she hadn't been naive enough to leave the safe, confining walls of her tower, none of the tortuous events would've taken place. Nobody would've died, her family wouldn't be in pain, and nothing would be wrong. It was times like these, when her heart felt like it was tearing at the seams, that Celestia couldn't help but think she deserved to be locked away.

"Celestia." A voice snapped Celestia from her tearful reverie, a voice that she recognized almost immediately.

"Mother." Celestia whispered back, following the echoes of her name. She slowly crawled around the cell, feeling her way around. She felt more bars and looked up; only darkness greeted her. Something cold gripped her shoulder, causing her to shrivel back in fear.

"Relax Celestia, it's only me." Her mother whispered. Celestia leaned against the bars, struggling to look through the gloom for her mother. The queen scooted closer, barely able to see her daughter's face. But she was there. Celestia stared at her mother, her tired eyes shed tears that spilled down her face and onto the floor. Although she tried to stop the flood of tears, Celestia found herself incapable of ceasing her cries. The worst part was, she hadn't the slightest clue as to why she was crying.

"Shhh," Her mother shushed her, gripping her hand. But even the queen had a few tears of her own.

"I'm sorry." The queen whispered, her voice hushed.

"We locked you in the tower without thinking. We wanted to protect you from this... from him, Lucier. But it appears he found you anyway." The queen struggled to convey her words, her tears dripping more rapidly down her face by the minute. Celestia listened nonetheless.

"For a long time we had hoped that Lucier believed that you were dead, but I realize now that he must have been searching for you all these years. The only way he could've possibly known that you had returned to the kingdom is through spies; we must have been betrayed by our own servants, insiders who alerted him of your arrival."

"When you were first born, your father and I confronted the evil king about his plot to have Lucier, his son, marry you. Back then we had no fear and our people faithfully stood beside us in that confrontation. But over the years, while you've been in that tower, Lucier has become stronger and even more wicked than his father and has seized many kingdoms and deceived many souls. Now I see that he has used his charms to divide our people and infiltrated our own kingdom. But we can't allow him to take it from us. We can't let him win, Celestia. Your father and I were thinking... if you can manage to escape..." Her mother suddenly stopped, alarmed. She had tried to rush through her words but she wasn't quite fast enough.

"I thought Lucier had made it clear... No talking..." said a voice from the shadows directly outside Celestia's cell.

Celestia could hear two pairs of footsteps echoing through the hallway. They bounded down the corridor until they stopped next to her cell. Celestia slowly lifted her head, wiping her eyes. She ground her teeth, glaring at the person through the bars. But before she had the chance to say anything, she could feel her mother's hand yanked from her own and, from the torchlight of the soldier in front of her, could see her being dragged off. Her mother fought against her captor but was unable to escape the grasp of the soldier. Celestia had just barely been reunited with her mother, and although she wished her parents hadn't sent her away to the tower, she realized that they had done it to keep her safe and knew they had truly regretted it. So, watching as her mother was taken from her, Celestia reached out hopelessly, calling to the soldier.

"Let go of her!" She screamed desperately.

"SHUT UP!" He ordered in response, leaning down and locking eyes with Celestia, her mother squirming in his grasp.

"You've got three days to agree to the marriage. Or your mother dies." The soldier whispered through the bars. A torch flickered on across the hallway. Where was he taking her mother; how would she save her? As worry clouded Celestia's thoughts, she found herself observing the lightened hallway. As her eyes traced the dungeon to the jail cell straight ahead of her, she froze.

Maverick looked back at her with tired, pained, and regretful eyes, blood trickling from his mouth. His legs and arms were bound and he was slouched against the wall. Bruises covered his skin and his clothes were colored crimson. His eyes were blank and dull, almost colorless. He struggled to talk but only choked up blood, the deep red being the brightest color in the dungeon. Even his hair was matted in dirt and barely had the golden hue it used to.

Celestia could hear screams echoing off the walls but couldn't quite tell if they were her own. She covered her ears and averted her eyes, suddenly aware of how much they stung.

The torch flickered off with the pinch of a finger, and the image of Maverick disappeared from her sight as the soldier disappeared into the inky surroundings. His twisted cackle echoed through the dungeon, the only trace he had ever been there.

Clueless as to how she could save her family and their kingdom, Celestia felt she should give in and tell Lucier that she would be his wife. Just as she prepared herself for defeat, just as she was about to call the guard back to give him her proposal, her pocket began to glow- flickering on and off. It heated rapidly, gaining the attention of the princess through the strong smell of burning fabric.

She dug through her pocket with her raw, clammy hands, holding the sizzling little ball of white fire in her palms. Its warmth and energy seemed to seep through her skin, running through her veins and pumping through her heart. It dried the tears that fogged her vision and dispelled her awful thoughts of hopelessness and grief, making her feel like Celestia again. Her mind and thoughts were overcome with clarity; she knew what she had to do in order to rescue all of the people locked in that dungeon with her.

Stroking the ball with a new found strength, a strength that didn't only seem to build her physically but to arise from the depths of her very soul, she looked at the darkness around her with hatred. Her father had died because someone, someone they had known and trusted and cared for, had betrayed them. Their very own guards, their very own knights, their very own subjects..

The orb glowed brighter, casting a light over the entire dungeon. Celestia's thoughts diverted to the illuminated figure of her brother, who lay in a pool of his own blood in the cell across from. Another wave of warmth swept through her, dissipating the grief, pain, and sadness she felt at the thought of Maverick. Instead, she felt... *hopeful*.

"We'll get out of here," She whispered, the ball growing hotter beneath her fingertips. She grasped the orb in her hands, holding it tightly as it began to soak through her skin and into the very depths of her soul, until Celestia was glowing from within.

"We'll save Maverick and his subjects," She spoke, fiercer. It was then that Celestia realized that she had done nothing wrong. That she would've never learned to love someone as profoundly as she had learned to love Abaven, Star, and Maverick, and she would've never felt the bittersweet emotions that came with being free if she had stayed trapped and constrained in those four walls.

She would've never found herself.

She would've never realized that her kingdom was never a castle. It was never a village. Her kingdom thrived within her. It thrived within the care and compassion that she and Maverick showed one another. It thrived in the trust and loyalty that she had developed with Abaven. It thrived in her veins, in the beasts she had tamed. It thrived within their spirits, within their whistles and within their memories. Her kingdom was never a place. It was just something she had to find.

And she never would've found it, if she hadn't jumped.

"We'll save our kingdom."

Chapter 27

As soon as the knight entered the dungeon, Celestia gripped the bars. Although she no longer glowed with the light of the white orb, she could still feel its warmth and power coursing through her veins. She felt as though all those years of struggle and isolation, as though being trapped in a cell, was nothing. And as difficult as it was to leave behind the old Celestia that grasped onto her own despair like a life-line, she had finally managed to release her wrists from those rusty old chains that had once held her so tightly.

The knight leisurely crouched down in front of her cell. Celestia slouched, casting her eyes tiredly toward the floor. Although she felt on top of the world, she faked being weak and helpless in an attempt to gain the trust of the guard. The knight set a tray of food outside her cell, waiting for her to snatch it. Seeing she was making no effort to do so, the knight grabbed a spoon from the tray and scooped up some of the mucky food.

"Here." He held the spoon through the bars. Celestia barely lifted her head, opening her mouth slightly and allowing him to stick the utensil inside. The knight continued to feed the princess, wiping a few drips off of her mouth ever so often. Once she had finished eating her grub, he grabbed a pitcher on her tray and poured some water into a cup. Reaching through the bars, he held it to Celestia's chapped lips and tilted her head as she attempted to sip the liquid.

Celestia knew instinctively that she could trust the knight. She knew, for a fact, that he was there out of the kindness of his heart, and he wouldn't hesitate to give her the aid she needed. Instinctively, Celestia grasped the knight's hand on her own, the power of the orb filling him with a feeling of trust and well-being. The knight set down the cup, holding Celestia's hands in his own. Feeling as though he could tell her anything, the knight began to talk to Celestia.

"Prince Lucier and his father have thrown over half of the townspeople in the dungeon because they refused to help them find you and your brother. My wife and son were thrown into this dungeon as punishment when I refused to kill my king, your father-"

"I can help free these unjustly imprisoned people. I know how to save them, every single one. All I need are your keys, your trust, and your loyalty," Celestia reasoned. The knight looked down at the keys clutched in his hand, and then to the lock that bolted Celestia in her damp cell.

He hesitated, uncertain whether he should trust and follow her. Taking immediate note of his skepticism, Celestia probed him.

"What is your name?" She inquired.

"Borin," he muttered in response.

"Borin, do you want to live your life knowing that you had lost your only chance to escape from the command of Lucier? The only opportunity you had to rescue your kingdom and your people?" She paused, finding him kneeling there, motionless.

"I am your only hope," She ended, knowing the knight wouldn't abandon her, or his kingdom. He stood, peering down at the slightly glowing, defiant princess and realized... there was no way he could say no. He wanted his kingdom back, and he knew that if anyone was able to save his family, who were imprisoned within the gloomy interior of the dungeon, it would surely be her. Although she had spoken only a few words and done little to prove such to him, he already knew. He could sense it with every fiber of his being. He knew he was in the presence of the one person who could save their kingdom. It was her, and she needed his help.

He could feel it radiating from her, the fire crackling in her bones. An eternal flame that burned so brightly, not even a throng of waves could dim it. She was the exact same girl he recognized from years ago, being dragged away from the castle with that same fire in burning in her eyes. Remembering that little girl, and seeing her now as the young woman before him, the knight was prompted to grab his keys. He slowly unlocked the jail cell, opening it as quietly as possible, a small creak sounding with the cell door.

The knight stepped into the cell, helping Celestia to her feet, placing one hand on the small of her back to keep her from toppling over.

"Tell me what to do."

Celestia looked around, finally out of her cell for the first time. She could see that the cells stretched on for as far as the eye could see, clouded with darkness and sounding with the pained moans, groans, and cries of other prisoners. She could see faces pressed against prison bars, waiting and watching. Families huddled together in the corners of cells, struggling to find warmth with one another. Men stared into the darkness in search of their wives. Women longed and cried for their children. Some prisoners bore the scars of lashes upon their skin and dripped of blood, others held their stomachs and listened to their bodies desperate cry for sustenance. Children held out their boney little fingers, feeling the air for something more than just prison bars. The elderly had collapsed, a stench following the decaying of their weak bodies.

There wasn't a joyous soul within a single cell in that dungeon, and it pained Celestia's heart, just thinking of how long these people could've been down here. How mistreated and awful their conditions were.

"We've been forgotten," the dungeon seemed to say. They'd been set aside to be saved another day. This was, undoubtedly, Lucier's doing. Lucier had kept his claws around her kingdom for far too long.

Celestia decided this would be the day. Freedom, it rang in her mind as though she could hear nothing else- as though it was the last thing she needed to finally push her to the breaking point.

Celestia glanced down at the large, rusted ring of keys in the knights hands and then out once more towards the moaning, groaning cells that surrounded her. She looked toward Maverick's cell, and could see his eyes, staring back at her.

Even through the darkness, she could see his eyes gleaming. She could see him purse his lips, forming a small smile of encouragement.

Knowing exactly what she needed to do next, Celestia lifted her fingers to her mouth, allowing a sharp whistle to echo through the castle. One she knew Abaven would recognize. One she knew could save both her, and all of the other unjustly held prisoners in those cells. There was no waver in her voice as she informed her newest companion, whose name was Borin, that they would not be escaping without protection.

Quickly after calling for the aid of her dragon, both Borin and Celestia worked their way down the aisles of cells, each with half of the ring of keys in their hands as they unlocked each cell as quickly as possible. They watched as daughters and mothers reunited in the hallways; including wives and husbands, fathers and sons, grandmother and grandchild, uncles and nephews.

But even with the joy radiating through the atmosphere, the people knew that their lives depended upon silence. No words were uttered, nothing other than the click of heels was heard. They could not risk being found.

They were only halfway through the cells when they could hear a single pair of footsteps descending into the dungeon.

The whole multitude of people, whom Celestia realized consisted of at least one hundred currently, seemed to freeze. It was almost painful to hear a breath echo through the hall. But as quiet as they were, the footsteps still echoed closer, until they stopped directly in front of the fiery princess.

"Oh, Celestia... Did you really think it'd be this easy?"

Chapter 28

Lucier wasn't a king. He would never be a king she would bow down to. He would never be a king that was worthy of being within her presence, yet he was an inch away from her face. Without Celestia agreeing to marry him, he would never rule the throne. The people would never accept someone who wasn't heir of the kingdom as their ruler, and so he was only a ravenous, throneless beast at the time. There was no one that could stop him from invading their domain, but even so, they would never consider him their king.

And although Maverick was the next best choice, Maverick was of no use to this evil, sinister man, and he would kill him to get to Celestia. She was the oldest, she was the strongest, and she was his only way of obtaining the throne that he so lustfully desired.

"We aren't quite finished with you yet." His smile was wicked, and all Celestia wanted to do was slap it off his face. She would've, too, but his footsteps had been accompanied by many more.

Soon the mass of knights and soldiers that had betrayed their kingdom lined themselves behind the grinning, evil man.

"After years of knowing you existed, and waiting for you, you're here and I'm not letting you escape," He whispered. As if on cue, soldiers leaped forward, ready to snatch Celestia into their grasp. Borin leapt in front of her, pushing them back with the blade of his sword. The rest of the mass seemed to surge forward, swallowing the evil, grinning Lucier in their midst. Citizens and villagers screamed, scurrying further back into the dungeon.

"Get Maverick, he'll know another way out," Borin breathed, pushing his weight against the steel of his sword as he pierced it through the skin of his attacker. Celestia nodded, sliding under legs and through bodies until she reached his cell once more. She slid one of the keys into the hole, jingling it in the lock, only to find it wasn't the right one. She hurried, finding another and glancing behind her every now and then, hoping no one would pursue her. Finally, she managed to open the cell door with a creak, but a hand pulled her away, into the mass of bodies.

"You aren't going anywhere, and we will make sure every last soul in this dungeon is lying motionless on this stone floor until you agree to stay," Lucier's cruel voice seethed. She felt as though his skin were grime against her own, and shriveled at his touch. She watched as the traitorous guards advanced on the defenseless villagers, pushing them to the back of the dungeon. The few who still had strength were felled, defenseless and innocent, their blood washing the cold, forgotten cobblestone floor with an unredeeming color of crimson.

As Lucier pulled her through the dungeon, Celestia felt as though she was sinking, being pulled into the bottomless depths of a dark and dreary swamp by a merciless monster. It was as though he wanted to destroy that faint light of hope she clung to, hoping to save her kingdom.

Her body felt like it was sinking, as though Lucier was pulling her into the depths of a murky and bottomless swamp in hopes he would drown her and destroy the hope she had of saving her brother's kingdom.

But, lucky for her soul, she had a match and she was ready to set a fire.

"Don't touch me," She growled, her skin glowing eerily brighter in the darkness of the dungeon. Lucier yelped, pulling his hand away and clutching his palm to his chest. He stared at her, fear flashing through his eyes, but then a sneer tugged at his lips. He reached for her again, but Celestia stepped back.

"I said don't touch me!" She roared, her voice echoing through the dungeon. Time seemed to freeze, and suddenly there was a rumble above, and she realized she wasn't the only one roaring.

The traitors, the knights and the soldiers, they all seemed to freeze, watching Lucier as he eyed his hand. Blisters covered his skin, and nobody dared to touch Celestia.

She took advantage of this distraction and hurried to Maverick's cell, pushing it further open and rushing to her brother's side. She could feel the energy coursing through her veins; she felt powerful. There was no moment of hesitation as Celestia unlocked the chains binding Maverick to the wall, helping him down to the floor.

He was barely conscious.

"You know, Celestia, I deserve to hang in these chains," He whispered, barely able to lift his eyes to meet her own. Celestia shook her head, shushing him and picking his frail body up in her arms. She wasn't sure whether it was due to her sudden burst of strength, or his lack of body fat, but he barely weighed anything. And, miraculously enough, her skin didn't burn him.

She would have never allowed it to.

Rushing from the cell, traitors lunged at her, barely coming within an inch of her to reel back, clutching their fingers and their hands and uttering curses and profanities. Despite seeing their co-conspirators clutching their hands in pain, Lucier's men still continued to lunge at her, creating a large enough distraction for Borin to finish unlocking the cells and for the remaining subjects to rush towards the back of the dungeon.

"Where is the exit?" Celestia asked, dodging past flailing arms and hissing traitors.

"There is none."

Celestia nearly toppled over.

"What? But Maverick-"

Maverick smiled slightly, his eyes lighting up laughingly. Just for a second, he didn't appear to be in pain, he seemed to be himself. In fact, he almost chuckled, but his voice was failing him.

"Make one."

Chapter 29

By now, every knight and soldier had been scorched or burned, and all but one had their sights set on retreating.

"What are you doing? Go after her." She could hear Lucier shrieking, and she pitied those who had to listen to him on a regular basis. Nobody touched her, they all just stared, parting like the red sea as she made her way with Maverick towards the retreating figures of the freed prisoners. Not a single soldier followed her with anything but their eyes as she moved deeper into the dungeon. Any who tried to follow were met with a searing heat, causing them all to flinch and cower away.

As the light faded out, all Celestia could hear were the breaths of Maverick and herself, and the footsteps of those who were trying to escape ahead of her.

She was surrounded by light and she could see her skin glowing in the darkness, a beacon of light that allowed her to avoid tripping and falling, a light that enabled her to realize when they had reached the end of the dungeon.

Then the cells stopped, leaving nothing but a mass of people ahead of her, all crowding against a brick wall, and Prince Lucier and his henchmen cowering at the other end of the dungeon. Make an exit?

Celestia could tell, by the roars echoing from above, that Abaven was awaiting her signal.

Celestia pursed her lips once more, a long and ear splitting whistle echoing throughout the dungeon. Within an eighth of a second, Abaven was tearing through the dungeon walls above the traitorous soldiers.

The traitorous soldiers screamed and begged for a mercy they never received as the booming sound of stone shattering and crumbling echoed through the dungeon, smashing their bones with nothing more than a clamorous crunch. Although many shielded their children's eyes or turned away as their traitors perished, Celestia could not.

Small grains of stone began sifting, landing on Celestia's head and leaving a trail of dust on her skin. Once Lucier's men were no longer visible beneath the piles of rubble, she finally managed to look away.

"Back up," she ordered, and the mass of villagers obeyed immediately. There was another boom, one that threw several people off their feet and shook the very ground beneath them.

Celestia could tell everyone was terrified, so she convinced them to trust her, to trust that she wouldn't rest until every last one of them left the dungeon alive. As the prisoners began to calm down, she stood and watched as everything around her fell apart.

Soon, the back wall of the dungeon began to crumble, brick by brick, stone by stone until shafts of sunlight pierced through the spaces in the wall, lighting the dungeon.

Suddenly, a large yellow eye peeked in through a hole that had appeared in the crumbling wall and Celestia felt immediate relief at the presence of her rescuer. The escaped villagers began to scream in fear until they heard Celestia shout, "No! He's not here to harm you! He's my friend and he's here to save you!" The villagers, feeling the sense of assurance that radiated from Celestia immediately calmed down and were soon assisting the dragon in taking down the last of the stones in the wall.

Every once in a while, Celestia would have to shout at people to jump away from certain areas, so they wouldn't be crushed by the collapsing walls of the dungeon. But not a single person was harmed in the process.

As soon as the dungeon had been flooded with light and there was a gap in the stone big enough for a single human being to slip through, the whole mass was pushing and pulling to get out. Everyone craved a breath of fresh air and the beautiful glimpse of the sun and the outside world once more.

As soon as Celestia stepped into daylight, her arms supporting Maverick as he limped from the dungeon, she observed the joyous people around her. They did not care that their kingdom was gone; they only needed each other. She watched as Borin reunited with his family and as villagers danced throughout the forest surrounding them. Everyone had a heart full of gratitude, and she could see it in their movements.

Celestia had desired the bond these people had with each other for years... she had only wanted to be part of a family. And now her family was gone, her father and mother, who she never even got to know, had been taken from her. But she still had Maverick, and he cared for her. And all those years that she had felt so alone, Abaven had been there all along. Loving her, knowing her, caring for her, protecting her. And even if she hadn't realized it sooner, she knew it now, and felt warm comfort start the course through her.

Celestia looked back, just in time to hear a muffled scream.

"Celestia, don't leave me here, please!" She could hear his shrill voice, and she flinched at the sound. How he had survived, she would never know.

She could see his eyes, gleaming in the few rays of sun in the dungeon. Half of his body was under a rock, his hands flailing, struggling to grip cracks.

"You're nothing without me, your kingdom won't survive," he spoke, his syllables blending together rushedly. His desperate attempts of luring her in to saving him, a man who didn't hesitate to kill her father. A man who wouldn't hesitate to take away her freedom, to disparage her and her true self no matter what she did. A man who beat her own brother, the only family she had loved more than life itself, senseless.

"Where..." She spoke, her voice threatening.

"Is my mother?" her eyes bore into his own, and she didn't need his response to know. Her mother was buried beneath the crumbled stones. Her mother had met the same fate her father had, and they were both nothing more than a pile of bones.

Celestia could feel Abaven behind her, could feel his breath whipping her dress. But she didn't turn around, she only basked in the comfort of her basilisk.

"You aren't going to get the kingdom; not now, not ever." She glowered at Lucier, who seemed shaken. He couldn't admit he knew she was right.

"Those soldiers... those knights that betrayed our kingdom to follow you? You left them behind in the dust. They were fools to side with someone who cared more about his success than their lives."

Before that evil man could utter one more word, the last bits of the dungeon's roof toppled over, clouds of dust arising as the figure of Lucier was erased from Celestia's view.

When she turned to look Abaven in the eye, she could feel a stabbing in her chest, could see the glow in her skin fading. Her work there was done.

Abaven nudged her and Maverick onto his snout, and, when lifting his head, hoisted her above the forest and the bustling crowd of rejoicing people. She watched over them, the small figures dancing around on the ground beneath her.

"Celestia," Maverick mumbled, instantly grabbing her attention. Celestia had come to the realization that even though she was the eldest, and new reader of their fallen kingdom, she knew that Maverick's heart was with the people; he was the one who should truly be their leader. Even though he was a man, destined to be King, all Celestia could see was her little brother. The little brother that had gone through everything and nothing with her, all at once. Finding no strength left in his body to speak, Maverick pointed out towards their surroundings instead.

She redirected her gaze, allowing her to see the crumbled castle and a shining, golden throne in the midst of it all. The orb, still in the pocket of her trousers, coursed with warmth. As she reached down, caressing it with the tips of her fingers, an image flickered through her mind.

There he was, sitting on the throne. His subjects surrounded him, admiration and respect evident in their attitude toward him. Maverick was their true king, and now Celestia knew it with certainty. She felt adoration overcome her as she gazed at that image and was reminded of how lucky she was to have Maverick and Abaven in her life.

Taken back to the present, she was greeted with the perfect picture of the setting sun, blanketing the world in a golden hue. She gazed out at the villagers surrounding her, observing happiness and relief in their mannerisms.

Not only had she found companionship, but family, as well. Not only had she freed herself, but the people of her kingdom, too. All because she had taken the leap.

The End.

Acknowledgements:

First, a special thank you to my grandmother Carla Laney for spending so many months editing *Breaking Ember* and helping me to perfect it. This book wouldn't have ever been finished if not for her and her support throughout the writing process!

Another thank you to Mr.McNamara and Mr.Cook, two incredible English teachers that I had when growing up. Both of them encouraged me to develop my creative writing talents and I wouldn't have ever written or published this book, or any book for that matter, if they hadn't instilled a love for writing in me. Thank you both for supporting me and my passion for writing!

And lastly, a huge thank you to my parents Leisa Waldron and Josh Waldron. They have always been the first to buy my books and the first to share all of my accomplishments. Thank you both for being my biggest fans and supporters!

About the Author:

Kadie Nicole grew up in a small town in Northern California, but spent many of her teenage years traveling the world with her family. She was inspired to start writing *Breaking Ember* by the various landscapes she came across in Europe. While the scenery was beautiful, Kadie struggled with her mental health during that time of her life. Much like Celestia, Kadie wrote this book to break free of her depression and explore who she was outside of the girl locked away in her mind.

Kadie is pursuing a career in Special Education and hopes to make an impact through her writing on those who may struggle with their mental health or who may have mental or physical disabilities.

Other Works by Kadie:

What Should I Be?
A coloring & story children's book

All For Him
A realistic fiction YA novella

Made in the USA
Las Vegas, NV
01 June 2024

90312984R00146